PRAISE FOR COURTNEY WALSH

Is It Any Wonder

"[A] pleasing tale of lost love, forgiveness, and rekindled romance…Walsh's wholesome plot weaves faith elements nicely as Louisa relies on her faith to make sure all is finally made well. Walsh will please her fans and surely gain new ones with this excellent inspirational."
~ PUBLISHERS WEEKLY

"A story of forgiveness, hope, and enduring ties that proves it's never too late for a second chance… Courtney Walsh once again shines as a master storyteller." ~ KRISTY WOODSON HARVEY, *USA TODAY* BESTSELLING AUTHOR OF *FEELS LIKE FALLING*

If For Any Reason

"Second chances and new discoveries abound in this lovely tale from Walsh, featuring a nostalgic romance set against the backdrop of Nantucket. Readers of Irene Hannon will love this."
~ PUBLISHERS WEEKLY

"*If For Any Reason* is a 'double romance' novel, beautifully written, poignantly sad in parts, but full of hope throughout. It is altogether a lovely book, with a strong Christian message and a really good story, and I cannot recommend it highly enough. ~ CHRISTIAN NOVEL REVIEW

Just Let Go

"Walsh's charming narrative is an enjoyable blend of slice-of-life and small-town Americana that will please Christian readers looking for a sweet story of forgiveness."

~ Publishers Weekly

"Original, romantic, and emotional. Walsh doesn't just write the typical romance novel. . . . She makes you feel for all the characters, sometimes laughing and sometimes crying along with them."
~ Romantic Times

"A charming story about discovering joy amid life's disappointments, *Just Let Go* is a delightful treat for Courtney Walsh's growing audience."
~ Rachel Hauck, New York Times bestselling author

Just Look Up

"[A] sweet, well-paced story. . . Likable characters and the strong message of discovering what truly matters carry the story to a satisfying conclusion."~ Publishers Weekly

"Just Look Up by Courtney Walsh is a compelling and consistently entertaining romance novel by a master of the genre."
~ Midwest Book Review

"This novel features a deeply emotional journey, packaged in a sweet romance with a gentle faith thread that adds an organic richness to the story and its characters." ~ Serena Chase, *USA Today* Happy Ever After blog

ALSO BY COURTNEY WALSH

NANTUCKET
If For Any Reason *(a Nantucket Romance)*
Is it Any Wonder *(a Nantucket Romance)*
A Match Made at Christmas *(a Nantucket Romance)*
What Matters Most *(a Nantucket Romance)*
HARBOR POINTE
Just Look Up
Just Let Go
Just One Kiss
Just Like Home
LOVES PARK, COLORADO
Paper Hearts
Change of Heart
SWEETHAVEN
A Sweethaven Summer
A Sweethaven Homecoming
A Sweethaven Christmas
A Sweethaven Romance (a novella)
STAND-ALONE NOVELS
Things Left Unsaid
Hometown Girl

A CROSS-COUNTRY CHRISTMAS

a novel

COURTNEY WALSH

Sweethaven Press

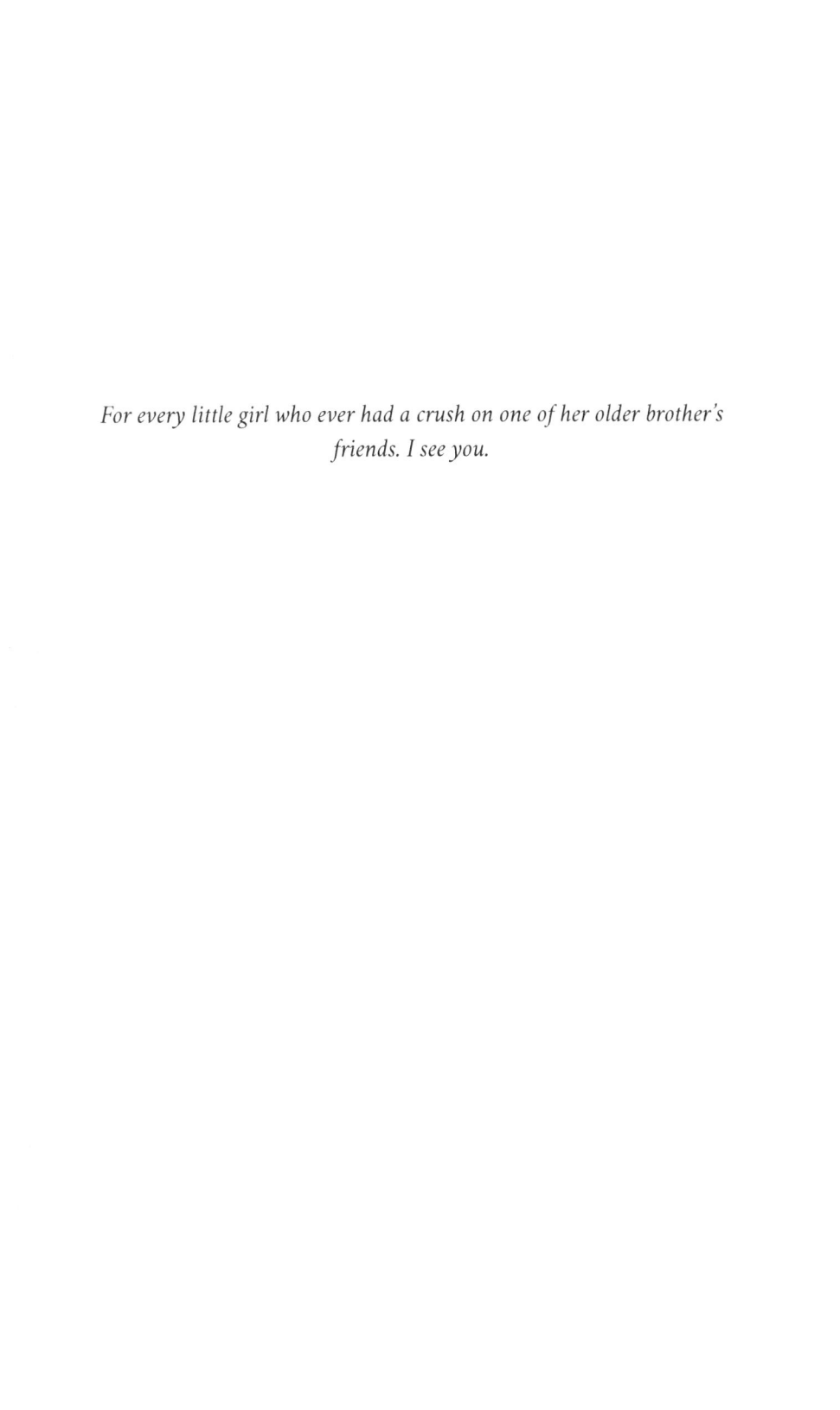

For every little girl who ever had a crush on one of her older brother's friends. I see you.

Visit Courtney Walsh's website at www.courtneywalshwrites.com

A Cross-Country Christmas

Copyright © 2021 by Courtney Walsh. All rights reserved.

All rights reserved.

Cover designed by Courtney Walsh

The author is represented by Natasha Kern of Natasha Kern Literary, Inc.

PO Box 1069, White Salmon, WA 98672

A Cross-Country Christmas is a work of fiction. Where real people, events, establishments, organizations, or locales appear, they are used fictitiously. All other elements of the novel are drawn from the author's imagination.

For information about special discounts for bulk purchases, please contact Sweethaven Press at: courtney@courtneywalsh.com

Library of Congress Cataloging-in-Publication Data

Printed in the United States of America

PROLOGUE

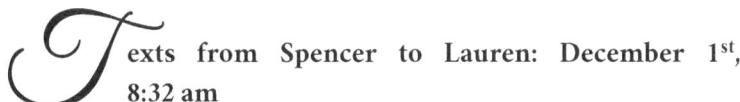
Texts from Spencer to Lauren: December 1st, 8:32 am

I know you hate talking on the phone so I'm trying your favorite mode of communication…
I figured out a way for you to get home for Christmas...
Since you promised you would—
Call me!

Texts from Spencer to Lauren: December 1st, 11:38 am

Are you avoiding me or just busy with your sitcom?
If you're busy with work, I understand.
I know you're really wanting to make an impression on your boss.
And fake people need perfectly decorated homes.
If you're avoiding me, knock it off, bozo. *<clown emoji>*

Texts from Spencer to Lauren: December 1st, 2:42 pm

You know I can tell that you read all of these, right?

Texts from Spencer to Lauren: December 1st, 6:18 pm

Lo, I really want you here when the baby is born.
And honestly, I'm not sure I can handle Mom and Dad for another holiday by myself...
I feel like *<Insert Gif of Stretch Armstrong>*

Text from Spencer to Lauren: December 2nd, 1:36:24 pm

Okay, Lo, way to give a guy a complex.
I'm your brother and it's Christmas and I'm having a baby and …
You're getting a ride home with Will.

Texts between Lauren to Spencer: December 2nd, 1:36:32 pm

Uh wut?
Heck no. I'd rather fly!

Really?
I'll book you a ticket right now!
It'll cost more than my mortgage because you waited so long *<eye-roll emoji>*
But THATS BROTHERLY LOVE RIGHT THERE, BABY!

Stop it!
Don't book a ticket…

> You know how I feel about flying
> *<plane emoji> <eye roll emoji> <puking emoji><tombstone emoji>*
> *<crying emoji>*

Thus, the ride-share.

> Nobody says "thus."

<Emoji with nerdy glasses><thumbs-up emoji>

> A bus then. Or a train.
> Do they still have trains?

For people like you who refuse to fly
<chicken emoji>

> Train then.
> I'll book it.

Or you can ride for free with Will..
I know you guys don't know each other well but he's a really good guy.

> I know he's your friend and you're my brother
> and I love you…
> But no.

Great so I'll text you the details on where to meet him?

> NOOOOO
> I'll find my own way!
> I promise I'll be there.

If you're sure <shrugging emoji>

                        I do not want to ride across the country with your womanizing egotistical playboy friend.

<eyes wide emoji>
He's not really like that anymore.

                        People don't change.
                        Case in point: Dad

Fair...
But still Will isn't Dad.
And he isn't like that anymore.

                        I'll figure out my transportation,
                        and I promise I'll see you soon.

December 10th, 10:18 pm

                        Spence, bad news.
                        I waited too long to book my ticket.
                        I know. Shut up.

So, you need a ride?

Just texted Will.

He'll meet you at some diner on the Santa Monica Pier.

I'll text you the details.

...

Fab. Can't wait.

<eyes wide emoji>

CHAPTER 1

*S*pending a few days alone in a car with Will Sinclair was just about the worst way to kick off a holiday.

Lauren Richmond could not believe she had agreed to Spencer's ridiculous solution to her fear of flying. Sure, her brother had done a Mom-level job of guilting her into coming home for Christmas, but his plan on how to get her there was faulty at best.

"What's the big deal? You'll spend a few days road tripping with a hot guy, do your obligatory Christmas rounds, and you'll be back here before you know it." Her best friend Maddie slurped her milkshake, even though the cup had been empty for a solid five minutes. And a milkshake was not an appropriate breakfast.

"I think you got it all." The booth in the diner on Santa Monica Pier felt suddenly cramped with her packed suitcase sitting next to her.

Another slurp. "*Now* I got it all." Maddie pulled her feet up underneath her, sitting cross-legged, knees tucked under the table. She looked calm and amused. She thought this whole thing was "fate" or "magic" or "destiny."

Lauren thought it was ridiculous.

Maddie didn't know the truth. Not about this. Not about him—the "hot guy" who would be driving Lauren from Southern California to Northern Illinois in T-minus twenty minutes (or whenever he showed up.)

Heck, even Spencer didn't know everything, so it's not like she could really fault him for suggesting she hitch a ride with his best friend. If you wanted to get technical, even the hot guy himself probably didn't remember everything, but her memory was good enough for the both of them. Certainly good enough for her to know that this plan only made her hatred of Christmas that much stronger.

Lauren came back to the present and noticed that Maddie was still talking. "You had a crush on him when you were a kid, so what?"

She made it sound so simple. So trite.

If he was the same now as he was when Lauren knew him. . .the flirting, the charm—scientists probably used his smile to calibrate their instruments—would she be as powerless in his presence as she'd been ten years ago?

Stupid smile. Stupid dimples. Stupid Will Sinclair.

Adjectives aside, she knew the truth about Will, and that's what she'd be reminding herself of. Over and over again, she'd drill it into her head. She'd wasted more years than she would ever admit out loud pining over her brother's best friend.

She was a lot older—and she felt, wiser—now. She knew better.

Common decency didn't make him a good guy.

"Lo?" Maddie had stopped talking—*what was she saying again?*—and now stared at Lauren from across the table. "You didn't hear a word I said, did you?"

Lauren sighed and pushed her plate away from her. "This is going to be a disaster."

"Did he even know you had a crush on him?"

"Yes." Lauren looked away. "No." She groaned. "I don't know. I don't think so. I mean, I don't know how he could've missed it. I wasn't exactly stealthy in middle school."

"Middle school?" Maddie rolled her eyes. "Like, as in when you were twelve? Please. I bet he doesn't even remember. I don't even remember what I did last week."

Lauren smiled. "Yes, but you're really flighty."

That was probably true. Not the Maddie being flighty part, that was a proven fact—but the Will not remembering part. And, if it weren't for Spencer, Will wouldn't even know Lauren existed.

"It. . .wasn't *just* middle school." She winced. "It was all through high school and even a little bit in college."

"That is the most Lauren Richmond thing I've ever heard." The bell over the door jingled, and Lauren's eyes darted to the entrance. Her heart skipped a beat, and she inadvertently gasped.

"Wow." Maddie shook her head. "You're kind of a mess."

"Sorry," Lauren said. "I don't want to go. Like, not just with him, but at all. You know how I feel about Christmas. And my parents. And traveling. Do you think it's too late to back out? I could tell them I have too much work. That's not a lie." She'd been working so hard, and she finally felt like she was making some progress with her boss. It really *was* a terrible time to leave.

Never mind that her boss had insisted she go. Sitcom set decorators apparently needed holidays too. Whether they wanted them or not.

Maddie shrugged and jabbed her fork into a piece of omelet from Lauren's abandoned plate. "I mean," mouth half full, "do you really want to tell Spencer you're not coming?"

Lauren groaned. *No*, she thought, like a little kid being asked a question they already knew the answer to. She did *not* want to tell Spencer she wasn't coming. She couldn't do that to him, and she knew it. Not only had she left him alone to navigate the ongoing civil war between their parents, but his wife was about to give birth any day now. Spencer and Helen were counting on Lauren being there to meet her first niece or nephew. Despite the impending road trip from hell, Lauren really didn't want to miss it.

Besides, it had been three years since she'd been home for Christmas. Spencer would disown her if she tried to stretch out her hiatus from her family any longer. She'd left him squarely in the middle of her parents' unending feud, like silly putty being pulled back and forth between them in an unfair game with no winner.

"Spencer was really sweet to set up this ride for you in the first place," Maddie said. "He misses you. I wish my brother missed me, but he's so stoned most of the time I don't think he even remembers he has a sister." Maddie's wild hair poked out from behind the sunglasses she'd stuck on top of her head. Her nose piercing glimmered in the sunlight streaming through the window.

"Do you want to come with?" Lauren asked. "That would make the whole thing more bearable."

"Yeah, I feel super sorry for you that you have to be locked in a car with a guy that looks like Chris Evans *after* the super soldier serum."

"Maddie."

"Are you going to almost touch his sweaty pecs like Peggy Carter did? Because I think you should almost touch his sweaty pecs like Peggy Carter did." Maddie waggled her eyebrows.

"You're not helping," Lauren said. The last thing she needed to be reminded of was what Will looked like. As if she'd forgotten. As if she would ever forget.

The door swung open and Maddie let out an audible gasp.

"He's here, isn't he?"

"If I hadn't promised Dylan I'd meet his parents this Christmas, I'd be in that car so fast the Olympics would have to pin a number on me."

"Wipe your mouth, you're drooling. What would Dylan's mother think?"

She shrugged, still looking at the door. "Maybe he's different."

"People don't change, Maddie," Lauren said.

She looked right at Lauren. "Sometimes they do," she said. "And considering what he looks like, *you might want to give him the benefit of the doubt.*" She paused. "He's looking around, Lo. Wave or something."

Lauren's stomach rolled over. She couldn't bring herself to face him. The humiliation of the last time she saw him was so fresh it haunted her. And it had been years ago.

He probably doesn't even remember. The words did little to comfort her. Yes, he'd been very drunk, but still—how could she assume he'd so easily forgotten something that had stuck with her so vividly?

"Hey, Will!" Maddie stood up and waved both hands, got his attention, and mouthed the words, *Over here!* while pointing at Lauren.

If Lauren could've burned a hole through Maddie's face with a stare, she would've.

Maddie sat back down grinning open-mouthed, like her face was giving a thumbs-up. She reached across the table and put a hand on Lauren's. "Even if he hasn't changed, you have. You're not that kid anymore, Lo. You're a smart, intelligent, successful woman—who just happens to be terrified of flying."

Lauren rolled in her lower lip as Maddie's words sunk in, followed by a wave of conviction. "You know what? You're right. I am all of those things. I'm not the girl who used to kiss her pillow and pretend it was Will Sinclair."

Maddie's jaw went slack as she looked over Lauren's shoulder.

Oh, no. He's right behind me.

Lauren's heart raced like a dog in a house with an Amazon Prime truck pulling up outside. Heat crawled up her neck to her cheeks.

"Uh, Lauren?" The voice behind her stirred all the memories, the embarrassment of years of torch-carrying. The rejection. The foolish way she used to make up stories about how Will had to keep his true feelings for her a secret because of his friendship with her brother.

It all seemed so stupid now. She'd been such a fool!

She'd learned the truth about Will a long time ago—he was the same as everyone else. He couldn't be trusted.

She turned toward the voice and threatened her heart to stop skipping beats, so help her God.

It would definitely be easier to remember why she hated him if he didn't look like *that*.

As was customary with men, Will had only gotten better looking with age. He'd filled out, and according to a recent text from Spencer, he was coaching collegiate baseball. Must be one of those coaches who worked out with his players. She paused for a minute to let herself imagine what he looked like with his shirt off. How well-defined *was* his six-pack and what would it feel like under her fingers?

And how had Peggy Carter resisted the temptation to find out?

"Lo," Maddie kicked her under the table, and Lauren realized she was staring.

She cleared her throat. "Hey, Will."

He smiled. *Darn that dimple.* "You grew up."

"Uh, yes," Lauren fumbled with her words. "I take it you work out. . .uh. . .I'm glad you were able to work this out, this trip. . .out." She pointed a finger at him, praying it would stop her mouth from flapping.

Mortification. Heat-flushed cheeks. Sweaty palms. *Keep it together, Lauren.*

She felt—not saw—Maddie's horrified wide-eyed gaze on her.

"Yep! Timing worked out great."

Lauren gave her friend what she hoped was a clear S.O.S.

"Isn't she gorgeous?" Maddie blurted. "And smart and successful and—did you know she's a set decorator on a sitcom? And an artist? But not one of those froofy artists who eat rocks and live off the land. Like, a real artist. She's going to win an Emmy one day, just you wait. But you probably know all of this."

So, Maddie must've interpreted her S.O.S. as *Humiliate me further, please, I haven't done a good enough job of that myself.* Lauren kicked Maddie under the table. She didn't even flinch. "I'm Maddie, the best friend."

Will laughed. "I like you already, Maddie." He leaned in closer to her, as if talking about Lauren like she wasn't there, *"And I did kind of already know that about Little Richmond, but thanks for letting me know."*

To Lauren, now undoubtedly beet red, "Are these your bags?" He glanced at the suitcase and bag sitting in their booth.

"Yeah," she said, still flushed. "I'm an over-packer, so it's kind of a lot. It's part of why I don't fly—I don't want to find out my bag is overweight and then—*whoops!*—have to open it up and remove my underwear on the floor of the airport or whatever. So, I just kind of threw everything in, and this really wasn't my idea, you know, to go home for Christmas and especially not to ride with you..."

Shut up shut up shut up shut up

"...and I can get them myself." Lauren stared at the floor, a trail of her word vomit begging to be wiped up. This was her worst nightmare, coming true.

"I don't mind." He reached for them, but she put a possessive hand out, stopping him.

"No," she snapped, "I got it."

She wasn't about to let Will Sinclair be the nice guy.

Maddie's gaze fell to her empty plate. Lauren knew she wasn't exactly being cordial, but Maddie didn't understand, she didn't know the history—or the truth—that he deserved every bit of her malice. And it was safer this way. Her heart couldn't be trusted where Will was concerned.

"Okay." He held up both hands in surrender. An awkward pause filled the space around their table. Then he shrugged. "I'll head out and start the car, I guess. Just meet me in the parking lot when you're ready to go? It's the black Jeep Grand Cherokee."

She nodded and smiled a polite smile, the kind you give a person who'd just budged the line at the grocery store, and he walked away. She glanced over to find her best friend staring at her from across the table.

Lauren looked back, defensive. "What?"

"Is that really how you're going to act for the next three days? He's doing something nice for you by letting your scared butt tag along in his car."

Lauren stood. "Don't get confused, Maddie. Will Sinclair is *not* a nice guy. Not when we were kids and not when we were in college and certainly not now."

"So, your plan is to be rude the entire time."

"Not...overtly."

"Well, that should be fun."

Lauren sighed, knowing it was time to go. "Stand up and hug me, or put me out of my misery. Your pick."

Maddie stood and sighed. "Nothing miserable about that man, that's all I'm saying." She threw her arms around Lauren. "Be good. Be safe. Have a little fun, will ya? You could stand to loosen up."

Lauren groaned and pulled away. "This is going to be the worst Christmas on record, so loosening up really isn't high on my priority list."

Maddie gave her a sad smile. "It'll be okay."

"I'll see you in a couple of weeks." She turned her suitcase around and gave her friend a wave.

"You know he totally heard you say that thing about kissing the pillow, right?" Maddie called after her.

Lauren groaned again and wheeled her bags out the door, where she spotted Will, leaning against the car like Jake Ryan at the end of *Sixteen Candles.* He wore aviators, a vintage wash sky blue T-shirt that stretched tight across his well-defined chest and biceps and he still, after all these years, made her heart turn over in her chest.

You are not that girl anymore! She repeated the words over and over in her mind and even muttered them to herself, not because she was trying to convince herself, but because it was true.

That girl, the girl she *was,* was only drawn to Will because he was popular, good-looking and out of her league. But she knew better now. She knew not to crush on someone for superficial reasons. And she'd also learned that she really was happy being alone. It was safer, after all, which she would be smart to remember.

People could not be trusted. They always let you down, and Will Sinclair had already proven that to her, hadn't he?

Which meant the only future that included him was the next twenty-nine hours.

And that was twenty-nine hours if she didn't use the bathroom.

She was determined to hold it.

CHAPTER 2

"This is your car?"

As Will watched Spencer's little sister struggle to drag the ridiculously oversized pink suitcase into the parking lot, he thought that after this trip, his debt to his best friend might finally be paid.

He then immediately noted that he could spend the rest of his life doing Spencer favors, and it wouldn't even come close.

"This is it." He pushed himself up off of the SUV. "She'll get us where we need to go."

Lauren glared at him. He hadn't seen her in a lot of years, but in that time, she had not only grown up, she had also apparently planted a grudge against him. He wasn't exactly sure why, but decided to put it in the "not my problem" thought box.

It was going to be an icy week, both inside and outside the car.

"I got you coffee." He hoped it would be a peace offering.

"I don't drink coffee," she said flatly.

"That's not what Spence said." He opened the car door and grabbed the coffee from the cup holder.

She looked away.

"He said you like the, uh—" he looked at the side of the cup —"white chocolate mocha?"

She kicked at something on the ground. "Thanks." It might've actually pained her to say that.

"Waiting on you." He opened the back door for her. "Here, I can grab that..."

"I got it."

Right. She had it.

She was probably one of those women who was insulted when a man tried to hold the door open for her. It was impossible to know how to act these days. He'd been taught to be a gentleman, but now that was insulting. And the last thing he wanted to do was insult a beautiful woman.

And yeah. Lauren was beautiful.

Not pretentious-beautiful though, the kind of beautiful that was understated. Very little makeup. Long, brunette hair pulled up in a messy bun. She wore leggings and a Rainbow Brite T-shirt that hugged her curves, which he took barely a breath to appreciate.

So, Spencer's little sister... not so little anymore.

A years' old promise to his best friend interrupted his thoughts. He had no intention of breaking it, either—no matter how curious he was about Lauren.

He slid in behind the steering wheel and watched her heave her suitcase into the back, along with a computer case and another bag. She pulled down the hatch and paused outside—in the side mirror he saw her put her hand to her head as if to say, *'what am I doing?!'*—and then she opened the passenger door and buckled herself in. She set her purse on her lap and fished out a piece of paper.

"I mapped out the fastest way from here to Chicago. If we take minimal stops and take turns driving, we can probably make it in three days. I also made a list of several hotels along the way and called to confirm that they had *two rooms* available so we don't, you know, have to share."

She said it like the thought disgusted her. He frowned.

She opened the GPS on her phone and started clicking around. "We can use my phone for GPS if you want, but I do have an audio book and three podcasts I'm planning to listen to, so would it be better if I plugged the details into yours?" She glanced up at him and her expression changed. "What?"

Start tap-dancing, buddy.

"Did your brother tell you anything about this trip?"

"He told me you were driving back to Illinois for Christmas, and I could get a ride with you."

"Yes. . ." he said, slowly, "that's true. . ." He paused. "But I've already got a route planned."

She shifted in her seat to turn toward him. "Really."

"Yes. It's going to take seven days."

Her face looked like when the dentist tells you that you have three cavities and *open up* because they all need to be drilled immediately.

"*Seven days?*" She practically shrieked. "What? Why?"

He really didn't want to get into the details about why he was taking this trip—especially not with someone so put-off by his being in her orbit. It wouldn't have changed her mind or her attitude about him, anyway. Time was, he would've used his personal pain as a way to manipulate the affection of a woman, but he'd changed. He wasn't that guy.

And part of that change meant keeping a lot of his personal feelings to himself.

"It's just something I always wanted to do," he lied. "Take my time, see the sights, go where the road takes me. Besides, this route is pretty famous—when it's all done, we'll have bragging rights."

Lauren started to respond, but snapped her jaw shut.

He handed her a book like an emissary trying to avert war in France. "I made a list of things to see along the way."

"This trip can't take a week," she said.

"It can, actually. If you don't rush through it."

The look on her face told him she was not amused.

"So, is this like, your vacation?" A deep, worried line set into her forehead.

"Yeah, something like that."

"I really don't want to go on vacation with you—I thought it was just a ride home. And to be perfectly honest, I don't want to go home either, so this is, you know, a lot." He thought she might hyperventilate. "Who takes a road trip in December? That doesn't even make sense." She was talking to herself now. "Why wouldn't you do this in June or July or any time other than Christmas?"

"I'm a baseball coach," he said. "Hard to vacation during the season." And, if what his dad had told him was true, it was now or never to get this trip done.

She paused, and he couldn't help but wonder what was going on in her mind.

"But you're going on a vacation alone?" She sounded genuinely confused—baffled that he would do something she considered so strange.

"Not anymore." He smiled.

"Have you booked our rooms?"

"No."

"Figured out stops?"

"No."

"Made any plans at all?"

"Yes." Then, after thinking about it, "Well, no. The plan is to drive the historic highway from LA to Chicago, then drive the hour from there on home."

"That's the whole plan." There was disbelief in her voice.

"That's it," he said.

"I can't believe this."

"Oh, I get it. You're one of those live-by-your-phone, schedule-every-second-of-your-life kind of people, aren't you?"

Her brow drew into a tight line. "No."

He grabbed her phone, and her hand, as if by reflex, followed it, connecting with his jaw in a hearty *thwack*.

She gasped and covered her mouth with both hands. "Oh my gosh, I'm sorry."

"You just totally hit me," he said.

"I didn't mean to." Her eyes were wide. Apologetic. Dark, deep brown. "Are you okay?"

He rubbed his jaw. "I'm fine, slugger. I know this isn't your ideal way home, but I'm a pacifist."

She looked away. "I'm not comfortable with this arrangement. She paused. "I can find another way."

"Okay," he said. That probably *would* be easier.

She didn't move. Had he called her bluff?

"I can look up flights," he offered.

"No planes."

"Oh, that's right, Spencer told me you hate flying." That was an understatement. According to Lauren's brother, the last time she got on a plane she had a panic attack so bad they had to do an emergency landing. For a fleeting moment, he felt sorry for her.

She clutched her bag in her lap, looking trapped and miserable.

"A train?"

"Too late to get tickets."

"Dogsled?"

She turned to him, not amused.

"Yeah, you're right, they're probably booked too."

She lifted a corner of her mouth and tilted her head.

Finally, a crack in the wall.

"Well, you're here. Might as well stick it out." He started the car. "But you are *not* driving."

"Why not?" she asked. "I'm an excellent driver."

"I'm sure you are, but I like to be the one in control of my vehicle."

She glared at him.

"Or, you can stay here and tell your brother you're going to miss the birth of his first child."

"Sorry." So, *thank you* and *sorry* both appeared to be physically painful for her. *Noted.* "I was expecting three days in the car, so this is going to take some getting used to."

"And you don't like when plans change, right?"

"No. I don't," she said. "I'm sure it's hard for someone who takes off on a seven-day road trip with no hotel reservations to understand."

"No, I get it. You're super uptight and don't like to have any fun."

"Can we go?"

"There's something I need to do first."

"We are so behind schedule." She sighed, exasperated.

"We don't have a schedule," he said. "We're going to take our time and enjoy whatever comes our way. I'll teach you to go with the flow." He could tell by the look on her face that was like convincing her to eat chocolate-covered ants because they were chock full of protein.

"I'll be right back. I need to take a picture over there first." He ignored her glare. "Then we can go."

"What's over there?"

"The end of the road," he said. "Or in our case, the beginning."

She sat, lips pursed, unmoving.

"I'll just do a selfie." He sighed. "I'll be right back."

He got out, shut the door, and silently thanked God for a

moment of peace. This trip was already hard. Taking it with a woman who loathed him made it ten times worse.

But, even with Miss Baltimore Crabs in the front seat, he was determined to make the best of it. It's what he did, and it's what Spencer deserved. He'd never had a better friend.

He jogged over to the sign that marked the end of the historic road trip, a trip he'd taken once before all those years ago—before he messed everything up. Back when he took the people who loved him for granted.

If only life came with a rewind button.

He snapped a few quick selfies, and when he returned to the Grand Cherokee, he found Lauren still as a statue, staring out the window.

He clapped his hands and rubbed them together. "You ready?" he asked as cheerfully as he could.

She stuck her earbuds in her ears, tapped something on her phone, and turned away.

Oh, yeah. This was going to be a great week.

CHAPTER 3

ROAD TRIP DAY ONE

Seven days? SEVEN??! Lauren hadn't even truly mentally prepared for the three days she thought she'd be spending with Will, but...*seven?*

She texted her brother, hoping he could read how hard she was typing.

> Really?
> How did I end up spending my first vacation in three years with your idiot best friend?
> Did you know he's planning to take a FULL WEEK on this trip?

Did I forget to mention that?

SPENCER.

He's been talking about this for years.
Glad he's finally doing it. Keep him safe, OK?

> Oh my gosh. WHAT!?
> I can't believe you would do this to me!
> <mad devil face emoji>

Maybe you guys will be friends.

> <pointed finger emoji> <gun emoji>
> <gravestone emoji>

See you in a week!

> Have bail ready for when I murder my driver.

About an hour into the trip, Lauren realized she wasn't listening to her audiobook anymore. It had turned into evenly spoken words in the background of her focus. Will seemed perfectly content listening to nothing but the sounds of the road. Lauren's annoyance about this whole situation, however, had morphed into a hot ball that turned her insides to lava and set her teeth to grind.

She paused the narration and pulled out her sketchpad, mindlessly doodling as Will put more and more miles between her and her home. Drawing always calmed her, and she could use a little calm right about now.

She *definitely* didn't notice the way the smell of Will's aftershave filled the car. She *certainly* was not inhaling more deeply than usual. And she was *absolutely not* thinking about the first time she ever saw Will.

Not even a little.

She was almost twelve. He was fourteen. A *high schooler*. He might as well have been a celebrity on a poster in her room.

That was the year so much changed in her house. She didn't

know what to make of her parents arguing. Her body was starting to revolt and act weird. Her friends were picking sides. And most of all, her feelings, *every single one* of her feelings, were cranked up to eleven.

But none of her almost-twelve-year-old angst seemed to matter when Spencer showed up after baseball practice with "the new kid" who'd just moved to their small Midwestern town, Pleasant Valley. At least, not in the moment when she saw him.

Lauren was sitting on the front porch, reading a Saddle Club book when Spencer rode up on his bike, followed by a boy Lauren had never seen before. Usually, she ignored Spencer and his friends—they were so immature, and Lauren had never really understood why things like burping and farting were funny. But the second she glanced up, it was like she couldn't look away.

Maybe the summer heat had gone to her head, or maybe she just needed a reprieve from her parents' constant bickering. Whatever it was, she was entranced. A brand-new feeling, warm and embarrassing and intriguing and exciting, wove through her body.

They walked up onto the porch, and Spencer stopped at the front door. He was brave for bringing a friend over with everything going on in their house, and Lauren wondered later if he'd done that in hopes of forcing his parents to be on their best behavior.

The stranger glanced over at Lauren and when their eyes met, he smirked at her. "My sister had those horse books," he said.

"That's Lauren," Spencer said. "She's a *nerd*."

Lauren gave her brother the half-tongue-out 'you're such an idiot' look, then forced her gaze back onto the page in front of her. The words had gone fuzzy. Why did she suddenly feel lightheaded?

"At least I can read," she mumbled under her breath.

"Dang, nice one!" The new kid shoved Spencer.

"Pssh. I know how to read. I read all the time."

Lauren didn't know where this came from, but she immediately said, "See Spot Run books while you're sitting on the toilet for a half hour don't count."

The boys stood motionless and stared, mouths agape, for a full five seconds. Then Spencer's friend burst out laughing, pushed him, and staggered over to fall in the grass on the front lawn.

"Dude! Do you want the address for the local burn center? Oh my gosh that was amazing!"

Spencer leapt over and jumped on his friend, landing an elbow. Lauren watched as they play-wrestled for a minute. Boys were so weird.

"I like horses," the kid panted, sitting on top of Spencer. "They're cool."

Lauren smiled.

"Dude, you don't have to be nice to her." Spencer pushed him off. "Let's go see if we have ice cream—my parents won't even care."

They scrambled past her, and the kid stopped briefly.

"On the toilet. Classic."

He smiled at Lauren before following her brother into the house. Then he was gone.

She sat, shell shocked, for too many minutes.

She went inside—*but she was* not *following her brother*—and found them camped out in front of the TV, playing some Mario video game. She sauntered through the room and into the kitchen, where she grabbed a can of Coke. When she closed the fridge and turned around, Spencer's friend was standing there.

"Spencer sent me in here for pop," he said.

She held up hers. "This is the last one."

"Don't take the last one, Lo-life!" Spencer called from the other room.

"Low life?" He shook his hair out of his eyes.

She turned hot with embarrassment. "People call me Lo. Or Lo-la-Belle. Or Lo-Lo-La. I guess 'Lauren' is hard to say?" Then, loud enough for Spencer to hear, "*But soap Di-SPENCER thinks he's funny!*" She rolled her eyes.

"Lauren, dang it! Come on! He's going to repeat that now!"

The two shared a smile in front of the fridge, and it was the greatest moment in Lauren's whole young life.

"You can have mine." She offered the Coke.

"Oh, I can drink something else," he said.

"You're the guest."

At that exact moment, her mom walked in the back door, carrying an armload of groceries and talking loudly on the phone. "I'm starting to not believe a single thing you say, Neal," she said. "You've had to work late every night this week." Pause. "What do you mean it's 'none of my business?' I'm your wife!" Another pause. "So, it's my fault? This is *my* fault?"

Lauren glanced at the kid, who stood awkwardly in the kitchen, almost like he was afraid to move. He met her eyes, and she saw the unmistakable look of pity on his face. It was clear his family was not like hers.

Her mom was still ranting, growing angrier by the second, struggling with the groceries, when Spencer's friend took a step toward her and caught one of the bags just as she was about to drop it. Then, he reached for the other bag and set both on the counter. Her mom stopped talking for a second, glanced at Lauren, then back at the kid.

"Who are you?" she asked.

"I'm Will Sinclair," he said. "I'm Spencer's friend."

Will Sinclair. She repeated the name three times in her mind, as if to lock it in. As if she could forget it.

"Spencer?" their mother called.

Spencer appeared in the doorway of the kitchen.

"Why is your friend helping me with the groceries while you're in there playing video games?" Back to the phone: "No, I will not get off his case, Neal. Someone has to teach him manners." Then, to Will, "Thank you for your help. Maybe you'll rub off on my kid."

Will made a face at Spencer and Spencer rolled his eyes at Will and Lauren simply stood. They helped with the bags, then the boys grabbed the potato chips and clambered over the back of the couch in the living room and hung out the rest of the afternoon into the evening.

Lauren sat back on the porch, opened her book, and replayed that smile in front of the fridge while pretending to read.

Lauren didn't see Spencer or Will any more that day, but for some reason she still didn't understand, they chose to spend most of that summer at their house, despite the arguing parents.

Looking back, she decided it was definitely because of the overabundance of ice cream. And the extreme lack of parental oversight.

It only took one brief encounter (*On the toilet. Classic.*) for that boy to make an impression on Lauren that would last years.

Now, sitting in a car next to him, the memory felt anything but far away. She tried to stay focused on Maddie's reminder that she was not the girl she used to be, but when she glanced down at her sketchpad, she saw the image of herself as a girl staring back at her.

She closed the notebook. She wouldn't get her heart broken by Will Sinclair.

Not again.

CHAPTER 4

"What are you doing?"

Lauren hadn't spoken since they pulled out of Santa Monica, but Will wasn't surprised that the first thing she said sounded like an accusation.

He pointed. "I'm exiting," he said. He knew it would get under her skin. He'd given up on winning her over, but he wasn't going to let her get him down.

Might as well have a little fun.

"Why?"

"First stop." He smiled, saying it without looking at her.

"I thought you didn't have a plan."

"I don't, I just saw a sign for 'Big Mom's Wigwams' and felt a sudden need to check it out." He turned toward her and grinned. "This is called being spontaneous." He waggled his eyebrows.

"Are you serious?"

"Rarely," he quipped. "And I bet you can't say it five times fast." He tried it. "Big Mom's Wigwams. Wig bombs big moms. Big wig wahms moms." He chuckled to himself. "Nope. Can't do it."

"Are you deliberately trying to make this trip even worse for me?" She blew out a breath that fogged her window.

"Oh, Lo-Lo-La, you are doing that all on your own."

Her jaw dropped, and she did that thing where your face wants to be horrifyingly shocked, but it comes across as a crooked-smiled laugh.

"You did *not* just call me that."

Yeah, I did.

Will shrugged. "Come on. There might be some actual big moms there."

She held up her hands. "I'm stuck with a literal child for a week."

"At least I got you talking." He tilted his head, keeping his eyes on the road.

Her silence spoke begrudging agreement. It was like her mind folded its arms and pouted.

"Look Lo, I was just trying to make you feel better about the fact that we're out here winging it. I know you're more of a list-maker, stick-to-a-schedule kind of person." He came to a stop at the end of the exit and waited for a semi to make a turn.

"Yep, that's me, regimented and boring." She sighed. "While you are all about the *fun*."

"Nothing wrong with having fun, though, right?"

She shrugged. "I just don't think it should be a person's primary goal in life."

"Why not?"

"Because we're adults," she said pointedly. "Because there's more to life than partying and making fools of ourselves."

Ah, so she remembered the old Will Sinclair.

That's not who I am anymore.

The reminder fell flat. Some days, it was harder that others to believe it. Something about Lauren made him feel like he might never measure up.

Her phone buzzed in her lap, and she disappeared into the

screen. Will felt he'd made a little headway, but like a game of *Sorry*, was knocked back to square one. He glanced at her, noticing her face, the shape of it, and the curve of her lips.

He'd met Lauren when they were young, but sitting here now, he realized he'd never really known her at all.

The truth was he didn't like that she knew him before he'd changed. He didn't know how to navigate someone who was so unimpressed by him, so unaffected by his charms. It wasn't like he could flirt his way into Lauren's good graces—she'd see right through that. She'd had his number a long time ago. So, why did a part of him want to prove to her he wasn't that guy anymore?

Will turned into a parking lot in front of the obvious tourist trap, pulled into a space, and put the car in park.

If he couldn't charm her, maybe he could at least throw her off her game.

"For someone who used to pretend kiss me on her pillow, you sure do hate me an awful lot," he said.

Her face instantly reddened, and he almost regretted teasing her.

Almost.

"I didn't. . ." she shook her head, visibly flustered. "I don't. . .*hate* you."

He turned to her. "Okay, honestly, how hard was it for you to say that?"

She ignored his question. "Where are we?"

They both looked up at the logo of Big Mom's Wigwams.

She started, "Is that. . .a large woman's rear end?"

He finished, ". . .poking out of a wigwam. Yes. Yes, it is."

He didn't tell Lauren, but he actually remembered this place. Vividly. After all, how could he forget? Seeing a huge woman's butt sticking out of a tent at age ten? That was classic!

Will's eyes fell to the entrance, and he was transported back to the first time he'd taken this trip. When he was planning, he was glad to see some of the landmarks he'd hit back then were still going strong today, including this one, which was unlike any other diner he'd ever visited.

"And I didn't pretend to kiss you on my pillow." She stiffened.

"It's okay, Lo," he said. "We all had our crushes."

She squared off with him. "Don't call me Lo." Then she got out of the SUV and slammed the door.

Will took a deep breath before getting out himself. He walked around the front of the car. "Why do you hate me so much? We don't even really know each other."

She folded her arms, and set her jaw. "I know plenty about you."

"Really?" He mimicked her stance. "Enlighten me."

"Please, Will." She cocked her head to one side, almost with pity. "You're not that hard to figure out. You're *such* a cliché."

"I object to that." He frowned. "*Lauren*. Do you care to elaborate?"

She seemed to consider it for a split second, looking him up and down, and then said, "Nope."

Wow, she's gorgeous. She has no idea.

She turned toward the diner. "What are we even doing here?"

He pointed at the logo. "Do you even need to ask?"

"If there's a big fat woman in a tent in there, I'm calling the police."

"Do it. That call would make the 9-1-1 operator's day." He pulled out his phone and held it out to her. "Will you take a picture of me in front of this place?"

She mocked coyness and sing-songed, "Do you want me to make you a scrapbook, too?"

He feigned seriousness. "Do you *want* to make me a scrapbook?" Then he flashed a smile.

His smile flustered her, he could tell. She groaned and snatched the phone, but just as she did a text came in. She looked at the screen, almost like she couldn't help but read it. Her face changed. She handed the phone back.

Rosa: I don't want you to feel guilty, but we really need you. Call when you can?

He cleared it quickly and glanced up. The expression on her face seemed to say "Exactly. Cliché."

"I, uh, just need a picture with the sign in the background," he said.

She shrugged, resigned, but obliged. After she'd taken the photo, she handed the phone back to him.

He hesitated for a moment, then asked, "Hey. . .you aren't hungry, are you? This place has surprisingly good pancakes,"

"I don't eat pancakes," she said.

"What are you talking about? Everyone eats pancakes." He started toward the door, unsure if she would follow. She did.

"I don't," she said. "Especially for lunch. We don't all look like underwear models."

She said the last part under her breath, and he turned so she wouldn't see him stifle a real laugh. Lauren was feistier than he remembered, and she was feisty to begin with. He kind of liked it. Refreshing, having someone say exactly what they're thinking.

And oddly, he was starting to like that his charm seemed to have no effect on her.

He held the door open for her, then waited in anticipation for her reaction to the interior of Big Mom's Wigwam Diner and Café.

The décor was an assault on their eyes. Camping paraphernalia and dreamcatchers and southwest style rugs had been hung haphazardly all over the walls, leaving virtually no trace of the cream-colored background. It was as if every person who'd ever eaten there had left behind a memento, and nothing about it was remotely cohesive.

On the back wall of the space, was a large wigwam, sides rolled open to reveal the door to the kitchen—and over the top of that door—a very ample, three-dimensional woman's behind.

Just like he remembered.

"Maybe you'll get an idea for your next set?" Will smirked over at her, but Lauren's wide eyes held no amusement.

"You want to *eat* here?" She turned toward him. "It doesn't exactly seem clean."

"Oh, come on, live a little." He led them to a booth next to the front window, and after sitting, Lauren immediately hid behind the menu.

"You know, we should probably try to get to know each other a little," he said.

"Why?" Her voice came from behind the giant laminated booklet.

"We're going to be traveling together for a week. Well," he added, "at *least* a week."

She snapped the menu down. "What do you mean 'at least' a week?"

He shrugged. "Crazy things can happen on the road. Generously sized women in tepees could pop up anywhere, you know. I'm keeping all of our options open."

She sighed heavily and retreated again behind the menu.

There was an awkward silence.

"Did Spencer ever tell you about the time we road tripped down to Florida for spring break?"

"No," she said.

He grinned at the memory, "Yeah it was nuts, we ended up. . ."

He stopped, and felt his smile fade. On the trip he'd gotten so drunk one night that Spencer had to carry him home. Not worth reliving. ". . .getting, uh, lost, we were wandering around for hours. We got turned around more times than I can count."

Lauren stared at him, her eyebrows pinched. "That's a great story, Will."

The waitress, a pretty blonde about Lauren's age whose wigwam-shaped nametag said "Melinda", stopped by their table. She gave Will a once-over, then smiled her approval. Her bright red lips matched her Santa hat. "Well, good morning, handsome. Haven't seen you in here before."

Will knew that Big Mom's was off the beaten path, not on the more famous part of the route that traveled from Southern California to Chicago, so it was unlikely the staff was used to anything but locals. Thankfully the trip Will took as a kid didn't stick to interstates and highways. His best memories always happened when he didn't follow the map.

"Haven't been here in a lot of years, Melinda." He flashed her a smile.

She pressed her lips together and widened her eyes. "What brings you to my little neck of the woods?"

"We're taking a road trip. Heading home for Christmas," he said.

"Ahh, and where's home?"

"Northern Illinois. A little town called Pleasant Valley."

She giggled. "Sounds *pleasant*."

Will laughed politely.

"And such a *long* drive!" She put a hand on Will's shoulder. "I'll be sure to send you off with a full belly. Everyone comes in for the pancakes," she leaned in closer to him, almost whispering, "but I recommend the French toast."

Will mimicked her tone. "Well, then, I'll have to try the French toast." He laughed, and she approved. "With coffee and a glass of orange juice."

She smiled again.

Only then did he notice the death glare coming at him from

across the table. Lauren sat, menu down, one brow quirked as if to make a point. Melinda hadn't even acknowledged her.

"Oh! What did you want, Lauren?" he asked.

"Burger and fries," she said, without looking at the waitress. "And a Coke."

Melinda scribbled the order on her notepad. "Great, I'll be right back with your drinks." She winked at him and sashayed away, leaving him to face his biggest fan.

Lauren shook her head slowly.

"What?" Will asked.

"*Such* a cliché," she said.

And unfortunately, he was pretty sure she had a point.

CHAPTER 5

Under different circumstances—namely the company—Lauren might've enjoyed her meal at this bizarre diner in the middle of nowhere. Christmas lights in the shape of cacti were strung up around the window that led to the kitchen, and there were actual socks hung from the counter in front of it, each with a name like "Ned," "Charlene," "Big Mom's Momma," Sharpie'd on the fronts of them. Make-shift stockings, of course. "All I Want for Christmas Is You" rung out on the speakers overhead, but a cover of it played by what sounded like a Mariachi band.

Lauren preferred this version to the original, and she had to admit, the burger was pretty darn good.

But the man-child sitting across from her—and the ridiculously flirty waitress—were enough to ruin the whole experience.

Melinda came back with the drinks and eventually their food. She brightened when Will, ever the flirt, *ooh'd* and *ahh'd* at his French toast.

"Melinda, you're the best!" He brandished his fork.

She threw a smile at him, barely glanced at Lauren, then disappeared behind the counter.

Will seemed oblivious to the fact that Lauren was almost completely invisible to this woman. In fact, as predicted, he seemed to revel in the attention. Will was the kind of guy that couldn't help but make himself known, at least to women. He relished in the fact that they were drawn to him.

As she ate, (*good lord, her food was shockingly good*) she watched Will. She couldn't believe Spencer had suggested she might actually be friends with the guy. As if Will were capable of being 'just friends' with anyone of the opposite sex.

Though, let's be honest, if there were a woman he could be strictly platonic with, it would most likely be me.

"What if you and I were a couple?" She asked after Melinda was out of earshot. Even suggesting it made her feel exposed.

Will grinned. "Are you asking me out?"

Lauren's face heated. "I'm talking about that *woman*. Our waitress."

"Melinda?"

She rolled her eyes. "Yes, Melinda. She has no idea what our relationship is, and she's been flirting with you since we walked in." Was it that obvious there was no way the two of them were a couple?

He stuffed a giant bite of French toast into his mouth. "Are you jealous?"

Before she could even fully register his food-muffled words, he'd shoveled in yet another bite before the first one was even chewed.

"Hardly."

Liar.

"C'mon." He opened his mouth to show off the half-chewed food. "I'm a catch."

She had to bite the inside of her cheek to keep from smiling.

Darn him.

The truth was she *was* a little jealous that women like Melinda had such an easy time talking to men. Even men who looked like Will. Why wasn't Melinda nervous around him? Why didn't she worry about what he would think of her? She supposed it was easy when you looked like a Barbie doll.

By contrast, Lauren looked like Barbie's librarian.

"I'm sure she'd be happy to flirt with you too if you're feeling left out." The corners of his mouth turned down like he was talking to a puppy.

She considered flicking a French fry at him, but instead shot an "oh, please," look, then went back to her plate and her phone. No sense trying to make conversation with Will—she didn't have big enough boobs for him to pay attention to anyway. If this were an episode of Bridgerton, he'd be the "rake."

How many years had she watched him flirt with every girl who gave him a second look? How many times did she notice a group of girls huddle up and whisper while keeping their eyes on him? How many times did he talk to those girls one-on-one, like they were the only one in the room? He did this with every girl. Every girl, that is, except her. Mostly, she was as invisible to him as she was to their waitress.

No, not invisible. Just not worth his time.

"It bothers you." He set down his fork.

"No, it doesn't," she lied. "You're just proving my point."

"Your point?"

"That you're predictable. A cliché. You haven't changed a bit since the last time I saw you."

For a split-second, it almost looked like her words affected him—and not in a good way.

Will narrowed his eyes, and it turned her insides upside-down. "Explain, please."

But she was still hung up on his eyes. Why did they have to be such a bright blue? They looked photoshopped. And why did they have to be on that face?

For her part, she knew she was plain. She didn't make herself up or pay a whole lot of attention to how she looked. It didn't seem worth her time. After all, she had no real interest in dating. Maddie said she only dated "placeholders," and Lauren thought maybe she had a point. After all, her main criteria for going out with someone was knowing that she was in no danger of falling for them.

She had Will to thank for that.

"I'm waiting." He raised his eyebrows to make his point.

She straightened her shoulders and leveled her gaze. "Okay. Here goes. You love the attention. You want women to like you, and when they notice you, you kick it up a notch. But none of them really means anything; it's just a game to you. See how many women you can string along. Never mind how they feel, as long as you get what you want."

As she talked, she wanted to stop. She read on his face how her words affected him. But she didn't stop, and she didn't know why.

Will Sinclair had feelings?

He slowly sat back in his chair, looking down and away. He glanced up for a moment, chuckled a small laugh, then looked away again.

"I, uh...I guess you nailed me there, Lo." Then he quickly held up both hands in apology, "I mean, Lauren."

Something niggled at her conscience. She'd been too harsh. In her effort to protect herself from falling back under the Will Sinclair spell, she'd acted like a jerk.

"Will, I'm sorry, I—"

But Melinda was back with a refill for Will. She topped off Lauren's cup as an afterthought and didn't look at her once. But Will barely thanked her. Just asked for the check.

"You ready?" He stood and set his tip money on the table.

"I can pay my half." She reached for her purse.

"I got it," he said, his tone clipped.

She'd struck a nerve, and she felt terrible. He walked toward the cash register, toward Melinda, toward someone who was a lot nicer to him than Lauren. She watched the easy way he interacted with her, and jealousy heated her face and furrowed her brow again.

Why did I do that?

Will glanced at her, and she looked away. Why did she care who he flirted with—or who he didn't flirt with? She had her own life. She was an adult—a successful adult at that. On her way to a promotion. And she hadn't so much as thought about Will, at all, for years.

It wasn't like she was dwelling on her silly little crush. She'd moved on.

Why linger? Why care? Why not remain wholly indifferent to him?

She used the restroom and met Will in the car, expecting an icy reception. But he waited for her to buckle her seatbelt, then flashed her a smile. A genuine one. "You ready?"

She nodded.

"Thanks for indulging me," he said. "I hope your burger was good."

Wow, he forgives quick.

He drove through the parking lot, back toward the road they'd come in on, and Lauren felt ashamed.

It wasn't a fair fight when your opponent didn't even know he was in the ring.

CHAPTER 6

The rest of day one was fairly uneventful. They rode mostly in silence, which didn't bother Lauren—she listened to her audiobook and stared out the window. They stopped off at three different spots, which oddly Will seemed to have planned for. There was a little roadside gas station with vintage pumps, a "bottle tree ranch" which looked like an art installation of hundreds of colorful glass bottle trees sticking up out of the ground and the first ever McDonald's, which was now a museum that thankfully, they didn't take time to walk through.

She did learn, though, that Grimace is actually a giant taste bud. Who knew?

It was strange to see Will excitedly interested in something other than alcohol or women. It disrupted her impression of him.

Now, as evening approached, Lauren's stomach growled mortifyingly loud enough to upset the silence in the car. Will laughed.

"Okay, I hear you. Good timing, too, because we're stopping

up here for the night." He pointed to her stomach. "We can grab food for that beast."

She glanced at the clock. It was barely evening. They had several more hours of daylight and could easily keep going.

"Is that okay? Does that work?" he asked.

After treating him like she did, he was still considering the way she felt.

Still, she didn't know how to keep what she was thinking to herself.

"We could drive a few more hours," she said. "If you're tired, my offer to take a turn still stands."

"Nah," he said. "You'll love this place. It's an historic landmark."

"An historic landmark in the middle of the Mojave Desert," she said.

"Near a volcanic crater! Are you kidding me? We're totally stopping. You'll love it."

She glanced over at him, his five o'clock shadow coming in right on time. It made him look even more like a rugged outdoor model than he already did, which she found equal parts annoying and appealing. The thing that struck her most, however, was this boyish excitement he seemed to have about this road trip. She wondered, but didn't ask, what that was all about.

"We don't really have time to see the crater tonight, though." He shifted his hands to the bottom of the steering wheel, seemingly weighing their options. "But. . . we could go in the morning. Or I could just go, you know, before you wake up."

"Don't you want to get on the road early?"

He shrugged. "Whatever. I don't really have an itinerary, remember?"

"I'm starting not to believe you. You've known exactly where to stop at the last three places."

He shifted in his seat, almost like he was caught. "You really think I planned on sleeping in a crater?"

She let a small smile creep onto her lips. "Dunno, it kind of sounds like a place you'd sleep. Do we have reservations at this hotel?"

He chuckled. "It's a motel. And no. Despite what you think, we really are winging it."

Her stomach squeezed at the reminder. She didn't like "winging it." What if they ended up in the desert without somewhere to stay? It's not like there were very many places to choose from.

"We should be there soon," he said. "Less than an hour, maybe?"

She turned forward in her seat as a text came in. It was her boss, Lisa.

> I know you're heading home for the holidays, but we have an emergency. The artwork I ordered for the dorm room isn't going to work. Did you have other options you could send my way?

Her heart rate picked up as her fingers typed out a reply.

> Yes, I had three different mood boards with available artwork in my original proposal.

She forced herself not to be irritated that Lisa hadn't read her whole email, trying instead to look at this as the huge opportunity it was.

"Everything okay?"

"What?" She glanced at Will. "Oh, yeah, no, it's work."

He nodded and returned his attention to the road, which was good, because his attention on her twisted her into a knot.

"Spencer said you work on a TV show or something?"

She nodded as her phone buzzed.

Send them to me ASAP.

> We should be near WiFi in about an hour. Will send then.

"I'm an assistant set decorator." She tucked her phone back into her bag. "My boss, Lisa, designs the sets, but she's taught me a ton. She's actually starting to give me more responsibility."

"That was her?" he asked. "The text?"

She nodded again, though she wasn't sure he was looking at her. She still resisted being too cordial to him—they weren't friends, after all. But if he was going to ask her questions about one of her favorite topics, she probably wouldn't be able to keep quiet.

"Right now, we've got to decorate a dorm room," she said. "It's only for a couple of episodes, so we don't have a lot of time."

"So, like beer cans and dirty underwear?" he joked.

"A *girl's* dorm room."

"So, like make-up and dirty underwear?"

She let herself smile. That was actually funny.

She loved her job. She loved learning about characters and bringing their spaces to life. She'd always been artistic, and she'd always loved film. Somehow, she fell into this career that married those two passions, and she couldn't imagine doing anything else. She'd been working for years, and kept waiting for the day someone trusted her enough to let her run with her ideas.

"So, you're like an interior designer," he said. "But for fake people."

"Well, the people are actually real people," she said. "I mean, as real as actors can get, anyway."

"Ha. Nice."

She continued. "This job is about. . . bringing characters to life." She turned toward him. "For instance, a couple of weeks ago, Lisa and I were working on a single mom's kitchen. The attention to detail is crazy. You can't just make an empty kitchen, you have to clutter the fridge with little kid artwork and quirky magnets the character picked up on vacation and post-it notes with actual reminders written on them.

"The windowsill is lined with vitamins and pill bottles and a cup of random straws next to a sippy cup. You have to figure out where that mom hangs her keys and throws her mail, and —" she stopped. She was talking too much—way more than she planned to talk.

"And what?"

"I'm sure you're not interested in sitcom set decoration." She let out a nervous laugh.

"I wouldn't have asked if I wasn't interested," he said. "I've never known anyone who does what you do. Besides, you talking is kind of keeping me awake. I didn't sleep the best last night."

She wanted to ask him why, but she didn't. She couldn't let herself get invested.

"So, what's your boss need from you now?" he asked.

"Artwork for the dorm," she said.

"And you have ideas?"

She nodded and her mind wandered back to the mood boards she'd created for this character. Lisa always challenged her to come up with her own designs, even though they both knew they were probably always going to go with Lisa's. Twice, though, her boss had taken one of Lauren's suggestions. She felt like she'd won Olympic gold both times that happened.

Not that she'd won Olympic gold or had any idea what that actually felt like, but in her world, the two things had to be close.

Lisa was a great boss, not the kind who was threatened by her assistant having a good idea. She wanted Lauren to succeed, and if she did—when she did—it would largely be because of her.

This time, though, she had more on the line. The artwork Lauren wanted to pitch was her own.

"Maybe you could show me." He slowed the car, then came to a stop near an old sign with the name *Pop's Diner* lit up in bright red neon.

"Not if they don't have WiFi," she said.

"They do." He parked, nodding toward a row of tiny white bungalows. "That's the motel." Then he pointed to a small building that she would've assumed was an old gas station if it weren't for the sign overhead that read *Diner*. "And that's the diner. We need to get a picture here."

"We do?"

"I mean, I do. Can you take one?" He handed her his phone.

She followed him out of the SUV, where he positioned himself *just so* in front of the diner.

"Make sure to get the sign in the background," he called to her.

She snapped a couple of photos, and he jogged back, took a look at them, and puckered his lips. "Not quite. Can you get down a little lower, sort of angle it upward?"

She frowned at the critique. "Okay."

He seemed unfazed by her confusion.

Finally, she snapped a photo he deemed "perfect". She knew very little about the route they were taking home, but Will seemed suspiciously well-versed in every stop they'd made so far. She had to admit, there was a part of her that was super curious about the history of these places—they were layered with years of stories.

"Why don't you go get us a table, and I'll get our rooms," he said.

She agreed and five minutes later, she was settled into one of the tables at Pop's Diner. All along one wall were shelves of snacks for hungry travelers, and on the opposite side of the space was a soda counter with a long row of stools. After she sent Lisa her mood boards, she waited for Will, studying the retro artwork on the walls of the nearly empty café. A thin, sparsely decorated Christmas tree, seemingly inspired by Charlie Brown, stood in the corner, blinking colorful lights like knowing winks of joy.

The space was a little piece of American history, and for the first time since they'd left Santa Monica, Lauren took a minute to appreciate that. These weren't things you found online to manufacture character and atmosphere—this was the real thing.

She absolutely loved it.

Will walked in, and for a brief moment, it was as if all the oxygen in the diner had been sucked out. His eyes landed on her and she forced herself to exhale her held breath.

"Got our rooms." He sat. "Two of them."

She slid a menu toward him, willing her pulse to slow down.

They ordered—burger, fries and a chocolate shake for him, chicken fingers and fries for her—and their waiter disappeared leaving her to face another meal with Will.

"So, tell me more about your job," he said.

She'd half-expected him to forget their previous conversation. Truthfully, she half-wanted him to—talking about herself was hard under the best of circumstances, but around Will? Doubly so.

Still, discussing art and television and her job came easily, and she answered all his questions without hesitation. There were several times over the course of the dinner she almost forgot their history.

His dimple made more than one appearance as he laughed at some of her favorite celebrity stories, and when he asked to see the artwork she was sending her boss, she didn't even hesitate.

She opened her laptop, pulled up the mood boards, and spun it around to face him.

He studied her three variations of the same dorm room with a furrowed brow, like he was actually interested in them.

"Which one is your favorite?" she asked.

"The middle one," he said without hesitation.

Her stomach flip-flopped. "Really? Why?"

His eyes met hers across the table. "The artwork in this one is a lot more interesting than in the other two. I like that it's kind of quirky and whimsical."

She felt the smile tug at the corners of her mouth.

"What?"

"That's my artwork," she said.

His eyebrows shot up. "Shut up."

She closed the laptop and tucked it back in its case, excitement dancing in her belly at his approval.

"Is that what you were doing in the car? Drawing?"

She nodded.

"Don't take this the wrong way, but I wouldn't have guessed you were an artist. I mean, Maddie rambled something about that, but. . ." He shrugged, his voice trailing off.

"But?"

"It's surprising is all."

"Because I don't really fit the stereotype of an artist," she said matter-of-factly. She knew her artwork reflected a side of her personality she didn't typically let out. The side that wasn't completely concerned with getting everything right. In a way, art gave her a chance to play.

"Let's just hope my boss likes it."

"Does she know it's yours?"

She shook her head and dragged a French fry through her salted ketchup.

"Well, if you ask me, it's the clear winner." He grinned at her and a tingle raced down her spine, all the way to her toes. Maybe she could be a *little* bit friendly, but just a little.

She looked up at him, smiled a real smile. Instantly, her internal monologue shifted. Who was she kidding? She couldn't let herself be friendly with Will Sinclair! He was far too easy to like, and liking him would land her in a not-so-luxurious suite at the Heartbreak Hotel.

She changed gears, quickly, spooked at the betrayal of her own mind. "Uhh. . . I should go. I just got really tired all of the sudden." She didn't wait for a response, fished some cash from her bag, threw it on the table and grabbed the key to her room. "See you in the morning."

CHAPTER 7

❄

HALFWAY BETWEEN DAY ONE AND DAY TWO

A piercing scream filled the stale desert air. Will stirred, taking a moment to remember where he was and how he'd gotten there. Was he dreaming?

He sat up straight at a frantic knock on the door—but it was Lauren's voice on the other side that yanked him from his bed.

"Will? Are you awake?"

He pulled the door open, and a wave of panic rolled through him. "What's wrong? You ok?"

She looked pale in the blue light of the moon, her face a blank sheet.

"I need your help—" she glanced down at his bare chest for a split second, seemed to catch herself, then looked up in his eyes. "Hurry!"

"Okay." He ran a hand over his face, as if that could wake him up. "What's going on?"

She disappeared from his doorway, leaving him standing there without a shirt or an answer.

She then reappeared, wearing that same harried expression, and waved a frenetic hand at him, motioning for him to follow. He grabbed his shirt off the chair and rushed out after her.

She raced over to her bungalow, stopping at her door, which stood open. He pulled his shirt on as he came up to her side, looking at her to try to gain some semblance as to what in the world was going on. She trembled, and pointed in her room.

He peered inside before stepping in, and his mind got snagged on the sight of her unmade bed. With that single exception, the rest of the space was neat and orderly, just as he assumed it would be. The room itself was identical to his, almost more of a cabin you'd find at a youth camp than a motel, and certainly not luxurious. Wood-planked walls, avocado green carpet, and orange and yellow floral curtains—the seventies décor was so old, it was likely about to come back in style.

She pushed past him and stood next to the bathroom door. "In there."

"What is it?"

Intruder? Deranged mental patient? Serial killer?

"Spider. Huge. Furry." The blood seemed to have drained from her cheeks, and there was unmistakable terror on her face. He knew she wouldn't appreciate it, but he found this out of character terror adorable.

He stood straight up. He so desperately wanted to poke fun, but she was actually scared. Will walked into the bathroom while Lauren cowered, turned a circle in the small bathroom, and announced, "I don't see anything."

"No, no, no." She crept in, and pointed a shaking finger. "It was on the wall of the shower. It was *right* there, Will. It was huge!"

"Huge?"

"It had fur. It was the size of a small dog."

Will let out a laugh, then stopped, held up both hands as if to say 'sorry.' "I take it you don't like spiders?"

She shuddered and raced back to the bed, carefully shaking the blankets, tossing the pillows. "You have to find it. I won't be able to sleep until it's dead."

He smiled to himself and started helping. They covered the main part of the room, but still found no trace. "I think it's gone, Lauren. It probably crawled down the shower drain or something."

"*No.*" she said. "It's in here somewhere."

He scanned the room, hoping anything black and furry caught his attention so he could go back to sleep.

"I think you'll be fine," he said. "The odds of it actually getting into bed with you are really slim."

She turned, suddenly defensive. "People swallow eight spiders a year in their sleep!"

"Yeah, that's not a thing."

"*It's totally a thing!*"

Will tried not to find her reaction adorable, but he couldn't get over how captivating she was right now.

Her eyes locked to his. "You're not helping."

"What do you want me to do?" he asked, genuinely. "I'm awake now, so. . ."

She crossed her arms over her chest, as if she'd only just realized she was wearing pajamas, revealing more skin than anything he'd ever seen her wearing.

"You're kind of cute when you're freaked out." He regretted saying it the second the words left his mouth.

She pointed a finger at him. "No. No, sir. Do not even try to be flirty right now. I'm not one of your bimbos."

"One of my *what?*" Will repeated. "I have *bimbos?*"

She gave him a look that seemed to say, "Don't pretend you don't know what I'm talking about."

"I don't think people use the word 'bimbos' anymore." He smiled.

She clearly wasn't amused by his amusement.

And to be honest, he was faking it. Yes, he found the whole scene humorous, however, he didn't like that his years-old high school reputation had followed him here. Some days he wondered if he'd *ever* escape the person he used to be.

Not that it mattered. Sure, he didn't want Spencer's little sister to hate him, but if she did, it wasn't like it had any effect on him.

Except that it did.

Why, he hadn't quite figured out, but he wanted to prove to her that he was a good guy now. If he could convince her, somehow that would make it true. And some days, he still had trouble believing it for himself.

He pushed the thoughts aside and focused on the problem in front of him: Big, scary spider; Tiny, terrified woman.

"Do you want to switch rooms?"

Another incredulous look.

"I don't have spiders in mine," he added.

"You don't know that. It's the desert. Maybe you've already swallowed one."

He would laugh if she weren't so serious. "I guess that's true, but I didn't see any when I took a shower, so. . ."

She seemed to be pondering this scenario, and he could tell it made her uncomfortable.

"Or I can just leave my door open in case you see the spider again," he said. "You can run get me, and I'll come kill it for you."

"We. . .can switch rooms," she said, an air of vulnerability in her tone. "Since you didn't see a spider in your room, I can maybe convince myself there isn't one in there."

He stood. "You sure?"

"Yes, I'll be right over, I just have to grab a few things."

Pull yourself together, Lauren.

She shook her arms out and turned in a circle, as if that

could get rid of the squeamish feeling and the prospect of sleeping in the bed that Will had just been laying in.

She walked the length of the room, back and forth, trying to convince herself she was strong enough to lay down and go back to sleep.

After all, it wasn't like she'd be able to sleep anyway knowing she was in Will's bed. She was in for a sleepless night either way.

She picked up her phone and texted him:

> I think I'm okay now. Sorry I woke you.

You sure?

> Yeah, I'm just being dramatic *<eye roll emoji>*

Well, I'll leave the door unlocked, just in case.

> Thanks, but I'm okay. . .

I don't want hairy spider puppies to get you in the middle of the night
<puppy emoji> <spider emoji><screaming face emoji>

The image of his muscular chest raced through her mind again.

> I can handle myself.

I have no doubt…
Door's open if anything changes.

She really tried not to conjure up a reason to walk through his door.

Try to get some sleep.

<thumbs up emoji>

She tucked her phone away and clicked the lamp off, pulling the sheets up to her chin, but within seconds she started to feel like something was crawling up her leg.

Lamp on. Sheets off.

Nothing.

"There's nothing in this room. Go to sleep," she said aloud.

But even with the lights on, she couldn't keep her eyes closed for more than a few seconds.

She got out of the bed, picked up her phone, and started for the door. She glanced out the window. The light from Will's room spilled out in the space between their two bungalows. She grabbed her door handle. . . then paused.

The feelings attached to the memories of all those years she wasted loving Will Sinclair flooded her mind like a tsunami. She turned back to face the dimly lit room. Whatever her problem was, Will was not the solution.

She slowly took her hand off the handle.

I'm a strong, independent woman. I'm smart and resourceful! I don't need a guy to kill a spider.

She sighed.

Talk about a cliché.

She sunk into the little chair next to the bed, turned off the main lights in the room, and opened her laptop. Maybe she'd get some work done, prove to Lisa she was committed. But it was hard to focus when she swore she could hear furry little legs moving across the ceiling.

It was going to be a very long night.

CHAPTER 8

ROAD TRIP DAY TWO

As was customary, Will woke up exactly three minutes before his alarm went off.

Getting up with the sun had become a part of his daily routine. On the days he missed the sunrise over the ocean, he felt out of sorts.

Normally, he'd go for a run before heading to the gym to meet the team, but today, he wanted to get on the road. Last night, Lauren wasn't the only person who'd sent out an SOS. Jackson Pope, his team's star pitcher, had called him about an hour after the Great Spider Chase. The kid reminded Will of himself, and unfortunately, not just on the field.

Jackson had a mean curveball, just like Will. He could throw 95 miles per hour, just like Will. He also had a penchant for making poor decisions.

Just like Will.

And if Jackson didn't get his head out of his rear end and figure things out, his fate on his current team or any prospective teams in the future would be completely ruined.

Just like Will.

Will wasn't going to let that happen.

He'd spent an hour on the phone with him, desperately trying to explain what was at stake if Jackson kept going the way he was. But when Will hung up, he wasn't sure they were on the same page. He wasn't even sure Jackson had heard a word he said. After all, the kid had basically drunk dialed him from a party that he was planning to *drive home from.*

The thought of that infuriated him.

Something had to change, and Will knew he was the only one to help change it.

He packed up his room and planned to swing by Lauren's bungalow to make sure she was still breathing after her spider encounter, but after he locked his door, he turned around and found her trudging toward him across the gravel parking lot, wearing a pair of tight black leggings, a white cropped T-shirt and a ball cap.

Well, heck. She looked adorable.

He tried to force that thought straight out of his mind, but that was getting harder and harder to do. She was his best friend's little sister. He had no business entertaining the idea of her as anything other than that.

Besides, his promise to Spencer was years-old, but it was still a promise.

"Anyone but Lauren," Spence had said. "Swear on our friendship."

How was he supposed to know she'd turn into a feisty, independent, beautiful woman who seemed to have no problem making it clear how very little she thought of him? That fact alone should turn his affection for her around, like a lost car in a cul-de-sac, but it seemed to have the opposite effect.

It had only made her more intriguing.

He lifted his phone and snapped a picture, the historic café and motel in the background, dimly lit by what was left of the moon. And in the foreground, Lauren.

He looked at the image on his phone and zoomed in on her.

He took another screen shot of the zoomed-in photo and saved it. He put his phone away and watched as she walked toward him.

He thought about their conversation over dinner the night before. He'd loved listening to her talk about her job—she was so passionate about it, the way he was about baseball, about the guys on his team. Lauren had this easy way of putting herself out there, of hoping for more where her career was concerned.

He, on the other hand, was totally fine with being an assistant coach. It's about all he deserved. Not many people got a second (*or in his case, a third, fourth, and fifth*) chance, and he felt lucky to help lead a team after his bad choices had nearly stolen baseball from him for good.

No one to blame but himself. . .and not really what he wanted to be thinking about right now.

"Good morning, sunshine," he said.

"Are we ready to hit the road?" she asked.

All business, even at this hour. "Any more spider sightings?"

"No, no more spiders." She looked a little embarrassed.

"Did you sleep at all?"

"I don't usually sleep more than four hours a night," she said.

He frowned. "That's actually not healthy."

"Sleeping is unproductive."

He chose not to correct that flawed thinking and instead asked, "Hungry?

"No, not really," she said. "We should get going. The sooner we leave, the sooner we get home."

"And you're anxious to get home?" The question was pointed, and it seemed to throw her for a split second. Will knew a lot about her family situation—more than most, he guessed. He didn't blame her for staying away the past three years. Heck, even Spencer didn't blame her. The drama with her parents was next level—they might as well have been on Jerry Springer.

It had to have been hard on her.

Was that why she was so cold? She was dreading Christmas at home?

She looked away and fidgeted with her necklace.

"So... breakfast?" He flashed a smile.

She tilted her head, giving in. "Fine."

"Great! Grab your bags, and I'll meet you at the car."

"Can we just eat here?" she asked.

"Well," he countered slowly, "we ate here last night. This trip is all about trying new things."

She frowned. "And here I thought it was about getting it over with as quickly as possible."

"Am I really that bad of company?" he asked, playfully.

"Not when you don't talk." *Zing.*

He noticed just a twitch of a smile on her face. She hit his fastball right up the middle for a single. He wound up for another pitch.

"Okay, okay, I see how it is. Maybe next time you want me to save you from spider puppies in your shower, don't have your frilly pink bra hanging on the doorknob."

"What?! You didn't...! Oh, my *gosh*..."

"You had, clothes hanging everywhere in the bathroom. It was like a laundromat in there."

She was actually stammering, searching for something to say back.

Curve ball caught her looking.

"See? Isn't this fun?"

"You and I have very different ideas of fun, Will Sinclair." She smacked his arm, then turned, visibly embarrassed, and started back toward her room. She called over her shoulder, "I'll meet you at the car!" Then added under her breath, "Jerk."

He grinned. She was teasing. He frowned. At least he thought she was teasing.

Once they were in the Jeep, Will handed Lauren a cup of coffee. "It's not a white chocolate mocha, but it's caffeinated."

She still seemed a bit embarrassed, though only slightly. "Thanks."

"I figured we could put in some miles before we eat," he said. "Do you want to look at what we're doing today?"

"Does it involve driving as far as we can as fast as possible?" she asked. "Because that would be my vote."

He glanced over at her as he put the car in reverse. "Do you know how much you're missing in the moment by always wishing you were somewhere else?"

She sipped her coffee. "You think that I, in this moment, should *want* to be driving across the country with you?"

"No, only my *bimbos* would want to do that," he quipped. "But you might have fun if you relax a little."

She drew in a breath and let it out slowly. "If you were facing the Christmas I'm facing, you wouldn't be relaxed either." She paused and looked down. ". . . and I'm sorry about the bimbos thing. That was rude."

"An actual apology? I'm shocked by this turn of events." He pulled out onto the road, then looked over at her and smiled.

He didn't know Lauren. Not really. And yet, because of her brother, there would always be a part of him that felt responsible for her. She was important to Spencer, so that automatically made her important to him. And he quietly hated that she was dreading the holidays.

Holidays in his house were what he missed the most when he was away. He tried to get home every year, though this was the first time he'd driven. There was something about the way his family's house smelled, pine trees and cinnamon, baking and blankets and fireplaces. The whole space was lit with those twinkling white lights his mom loved ("The colored ones are gaudy! White lights are elegant!") and filled with the sound of family, of children, of Christmas carols. . . of home.

His family was also loud and nosy, fiercely close, and crazy competitive when it came to board games. He loved every single second of it.

And Christmas morning, he, his parents, his grandpa, his two sisters and their husbands would sit around the table in pajamas before opening presents, drinking coffee and eating the big, home-cooked breakfast his mother insisted on making.

Everyone should have that kind of Christmas.

Unfortunately, he knew he was the exception, not the rule. For Spencer and Lauren, the greatest gift on Christmas morning was parental silence. Too often, they were used as leverage in their parents' never-ending argument. He knew they were overlooked, an afterthought, or worse yet, bargaining chips... and he hated that for both of them.

He'd really taken it all for granted when he was younger, and after his little wake-up call, he vowed to never ignore that blessing again.

"What was your last Christmas like?" Maybe things had improved since she'd moved away.

She stilled. "I don't really celebrate Christmas."

"At all?"

She shrugged. "I don't like holidays. Especially Christmas. And I *really* hate my birthday."

"Why?" He dared a quick glance at her, but she was focused on the passing desert landscape out the window.

"Can we talk about something else?" she asked, suddenly cold. "Or nothing? We could talk about nothing."

He silently acquiesced. Her walls were rebuilt.

Will flipped through radio stations until he found one playing Christmas music. As fate would have it, it was "All I Want for Christmas is You," and Will started singing full voice. He glanced at Lauren, singing and shrugging his shoulders and indicating to the radio as if to ask, 'How'm I doin?'

She pulled out her Air Pods and made a point of sticking

them in her ears one at a time, then feigning serenity, slowly sinking back into her seat.

And that's how the entire day went.

They stopped twice for food—and Lauren spent both meals on her phone. They stopped at a general store, a vintage gas station, a church built in the 1600's, and drove through a petrified forest. Lauren slept, played solitaire, listened to music, doodled in her sketchbook, answered texts, and made a point of avoiding talking to Will.

And he made a point to pretend it didn't bother him.

He wanted her to like him. He knew this was something he needed to work on, his need for approval, but this was different. This wasn't about winning her over for the sake of his own ego—it was about winning her over because he really liked her.

I really like her. Like, genuinely.

Was it wrong that he wanted to be her friend?

Was it also wrong that he knew he was kidding himself thinking that's all this was?

Late afternoon, as he filled up the gas tank at a classic station, Will snapped a selfie just as a text from Jackson's mom came in.

Hey Coach, sorry to disturb you on your Christmas break.
I saw you and Jackson have been texting, and I wanted to let you know he was in an accident last night.
Nothing too serious, but we're hoping it was the wake-up call he needed to make some better choices.
Just thought you should know.

Will had met Jackson's family when he was a senior in high school and visiting Pacific University—they were good people, a lot like his own family. Even though Jackson's mom hadn't asked in her text, even though there was probably nothing he could do, Will looked up the name of Jackson's hometown to see how far out of the way it was.

Divine intervention? Maybe. If what Jackson had told him about his little hometown was true, it could be exactly what this trip home needed—and exactly what a certain passenger in his car needed to get into the Christmas spirit.

As the data loaded on his phone, Will blinked, then grinned. Then grinned bigger. As fate would have it, Jackson Pope's family was from a little town called El Muérdago. And *muérdago*, in English, means *mistletoe*.

CHAPTER 9

❄

*L*auren didn't need a lot of sleep. But she did need more than zero hours, and after the spider fiasco, that's exactly what she got.

Which is why she dozed off.

And why her little nap turned in to an all-out slumber—that crashy, deep sleep that makes you forget where you are—and who you're with. Her awakening was a rude one when she realized she was, in fact, in a car with a whole lot of miles left to cover. And behind the steering wheel was Will Sinclair, who was, unfortunately, turning out to be a pretty decent guy.

The sun had set during her snooze, and unlike yesterday, they were still driving.

Good. Maybe he'd gotten it into his head that they needed to get home, get Christmas over with, and get back to real life.

Or maybe he'd gotten tired of her salty attitude and wanted out of this car as soon as possible.

She shifted at the thought, and then sat up. They certainly weren't in the desert anymore. Even in the dark, she could see lush green trees and a light dusting of snow on the road.

"The princess awakes," Will announced, far too cheerfully.

"Where are we?"

"A little off the beaten path," he said, caution in his voice.

"A path that's closer to Illinois?"

He pulled a face.

"Will?"

"It's sort of an unplanned stop," he said. "Not too far out of the way."

She frowned.

"I heard about this great little town in the mountains," he said.

Her ears popped. "We're in the mountains?"

"Yes," he pointed, "those big things over there."

She wasn't amused.

"It's just a few hours out of the way."

"Wait." She sat up straighter. "A few hours? How many?"

"Just a couple. A few. Like three or four?"

"Three or four hours out of the way? One way or two?"

Another face. "It'll be worth it?"

There was a question in his voice.

She groaned and faced him. "Even you don't sound convinced."

"No, it will. I was going to wake you and make sure it was okay, but you were so cute, you know, snoring and drooling and everything—"

"Knock it off," she said lightly, but when she faced him, she realized he was serious. She'd been *snoring* and *drooling*?

"You know you talk in your sleep, right?" He waggled his eyebrows and grinned at her.

"No, I don't." *Do I?*

He tossed her a teasing look, and her heartrate kicked up. What if she'd said something embarrassing? Wouldn't that be par for the course? She wiped her sweaty palms on her pants and searched her mind for something—anything—to say. "What exactly do you have planned for this 'great little mountain town'?"

"So many things," he said.

"And it's adding how many hours to our trip?"

He shrugged. "Let's just see where the road takes us."

She chuckled, but not because she thought it was funny. She repeated, matching his inflection, "Let's just see where the road takes us?"

"Now you're getting it." His smile widened.

"That sounds like something you'd embroider on a pillow," she countered.

She could sense the amusement on his face, even in the dark.

"What's it like not to take anything seriously?" She tried to keep her tone light, but it didn't exactly work. She was annoyed. She didn't have an indefinite number of days off of work, and she really didn't love spending any extra time in this car with Will, trying to focus only on his bad qualities—especially since it was getting more and more difficult to do so the longer they were cooped up together.

"I take plenty of things seriously." He focused on the road. "I just don't take everything seriously. I guess that's how we're different."

She chewed the inside of her lip.

"You know, I can't tell if you're being like this because you don't want to go home for Christmas or because you just really don't like me."

If only that were true.

"Or both." He laughed. "Maybe it's both."

She stared at him, caught.

"But I'm not sure why?"

She turned away and clenched her jaw, the words she wanted to blurt firmly held behind her teeth. She hadn't expected him to be so forthright. It threw her for a loop.

A long, awkward pause hung in the air. Lauren's eyes darted

back and forth, searching for a reply that would sound plausible, a neighbor to the truth but definitely *not* the truth. How did she explain how awkward this was for her? Being here, now, with him? It's not like she could say, "Well, I have to ruminate on every negative thing about you because if I don't, I'm likely to fall for you all over again. Oh, yeah, did I fail to mention my crippling crush on you?"

She didn't dare tell him all the ways she'd dreamed of him and for so many years, and then, when they finally—finally—shared a moment, just the two of them, it was one of the biggest disappointments of her life.

And she was 98% sure he didn't even remember it. Or worse, he pretended not to.

She supposed that's what happened when you built a person up. The truth was, she didn't know Will, not really. She never had. She'd fixated on who she thought he was—made him the person she needed at the time. The reality was such a heartbreaking kick in the teeth, it left her feeling humiliated and ridiculous, and she needed no help feeling either of those things.

Maybe she was being too hard on him. She was acting out of her own experience without cluing him in. It wasn't fair.

Will glanced over at her several times, and finally said, "I mean, I get why you're not anxious to go home—and I know we were never friends, but I'm a pretty likable guy. This could even be fun."

Thankfully, before she could respond, a sign crested over the rise in the road—"El Muérdago."

Will slowed to twenty-five, then twenty, then fifteen. Lauren could hear the soft crunch of the snow under the tires. She straightened up in her seat and stared. . . El Muérdago was seemingly cut and pasted from the front of a Christmas postcard.

Tiny twinkle lights were draped through the trees surrounding a large lake, and all around the perimeter were glowing luminaries. The road took them into a well-lit area marked "Old Plaza," where people darted across the street, shopping, laughing, celebrating. A live nativity caught her eye as they drove by, and the store fronts boasted festive displays.

A Santa stood on the corner, ringing a Salvation Army bell, while big wreaths with giant red bows hung from each lamp post.

"Look, tomorrow is a torchlight parade and tree lighting." Will read one of the many signs detailing the activities that were apparently scheduled for the week. "Not sure what a torchlight parade is, but it sounds festive."

"But we won't be here tomorrow," she said. "Right?"

"I told you," he smiled, "no plans."

She groaned. She should've taken a bus. She hadn't because she didn't want to be at the mercy of a bus schedule, but, as it turned out, being at the mercy of a Will Sinclair schedule was far worse.

"Maybe I can catch a bus back home."

"You could do that, sure." he said. "Or you could open your mind to adventure."

She rolled her eyes as they passed giant, tumbleweed snowmen with sticks for arms; each decorated differently and sponsored by local businesses. A top-hatted formal-wear all-business snowman, a snowman holding a cordless drill and hammer for the hardware store, and perhaps the most eye-catching of all, a snowwoman wearing what appeared to be a biodegradable wedding gown.

"It's a great little town, right?"

She never would've taken him for a lover of Christmas, but he seemed downright giddy about this place, this holiday, and, if she was honest, about life in general. There was a niggle of jealousy at the realization. Lauren had never felt that way. Most days, she woke up focused and ready to work. A day without a plan challenged her, and not in a good way.

They turned into a neighborhood, and she could feel annoyance coursing through her. "Will, what are we doing here? If this is your attempt to try and convince me I need to loosen up, it's not working. In fact, it's having the opposite effect."

He stopped the car in front of a small, white ranch home, its outline strung with colorful lights. A blow-up Santa tilted proudly in the front yard.

"Sorry, I—" He paused. It was like he was trying to tell her something without telling her everything. "I just need to check on something."

Only then did she start to think maybe their being here wasn't accidental at all.

"Do you want to wait in the car or come in with me?"

"Are we on the set of a Christmas movie?" She glanced over at him.

"It could be. Did you know El Muérdago translates to 'mistletoe'? So, you might want to guard your lips."

Her eyes darted to his lips, lingering a little longer than was appropriate. "You brought me to a town called 'Mistletoe'?"

And why did her heart sputter at the thought?

He unbuckled his seatbelt, leaning toward her as he did. She inhaled at that exact moment and forced herself not to think about the smell of his aftershave. (It was really, really nice.)

"Did you ever think maybe this isn't about you at all?" He was out of the car before she could respond, but his words remained, filling the empty space.

He walked around and stood, waiting for her on the sidewalk.

She absolutely did not want to get out and face him. He'd simultaneously excited her and rebuked her, and her emotions were sloshing around like a half-full gas tank in a boat on the sea.

This entire trip, she'd been so ugly to him, and he'd never—not once—uttered a cross word to her. She was ashamed to think that this was how she'd been treating him, even if he was *Will Sinclair.*

In an effort to *not* fall for him, she'd forgotten basic human decency. Internally, she groaned. She'd probably have to apologize for that at some point. That was going to sting.

He bent down and gently knocked on her window. He gestured a "You coming?"

Slowly, she opened the door and got out. As she did, her foot caught on the curb, and she teetered slightly. Will immediately caught and righted her, and all of a sudden, she was eleven-going-on-twelve again, back in her kitchen, sharing a smile and a can of Coke.

He held onto her arm, reached around (*oh my gosh, he was so close*) and shut her door. He turned, and she followed him to the front door of a house of strangers. What were they doing here?

She didn't love social settings. She had a knack for feeling out of place. While Will was charismatic and a little too charming, Lauren was a wallflower. She'd grown quite accustomed to the background.

Would she be able to fade here?

"Now do you want to tell me where we are?" she asked.

"I'm sorry," he apologized. "I really am. I know you want to get home. This is just something I need to do. I promise it won't take long."

She was struck by his sincerity. She figured he could've dropped her at a hotel, though she was pretty sure they didn't have reservations anywhere.

What if he was visiting a girlfriend? Or that *Rosa* who'd texted him yesterday? How awkward was this going to be?

Get it together, Lauren.

But no amount of pep-talking helped her. She was in a strange town that looked like Christmas had thrown up all over it, about to walk into a situation she had no control over, with a guy who—despite her very valiant efforts against this—still seemed to have some sort of effect on her. She really just wanted to go back to California and pretend this trip had never happened.

Will rang the doorbell, and when it opened, an adorable, plump middle-aged woman squealed at the sight of him.

The woman's eyes filled with tears and she flung her arms around him and pulled him into a hug he clearly wasn't expecting.

"*Ah! Dios mío, es maravilloso verte*, Coach Will!" She gushed the words, still clinging to him. "I can't believe you came!"

"Rosa!" He sounded out of breath, she was squeezing him hard, "*¿Cómo has estado?*" She finally let him go, rubbing his arms, like his *abuela*. "It was hardly out of the way at all," he said, with a sideways glance at Lauren.

Rosa? This *was Rosa?*

Her face flushed, hot with the embarrassment of her assumption. Add that to the list of things she'd have to apologize for.

"*Adelante*, Coach Will, come in, come in." The woman stepped aside, and when she met Lauren's eyes, her mouth opened and she smiled wide. She slugged Will on the arm and said, "Coach Will, you didn't tell us *tu novia* was so beautiful!" She touched Lauren's cheek and looked at her in a way her own mother never had. Rosa held Lauren's arms warmly. "He's been keeping you a *secret*."

Lauren started to correct the woman, but she didn't give her a chance.

"I'm Rosa," she said. "And your Will is our hero." She leaned in closer. "And *so* handsome!" She grabbed both of Will's cheeks and squeezed.

Lauren saw Will's flustered grin, and she forced herself to look away because the whole scene playing out in front of her was downright adorable. Seeing him embarrassed as this woman fussed over him charmed Lauren in a way no amount of flirting ever had.

"I'm...Lauren," she stammered.

"Lauren! Such a beautiful name!" Rosa pulled Lauren into a tight hug. She looked desperately at Will who just shrugged, put his hands up and chuckled.

Rosa started down the hall, flanked by colorful Christmas lights hanging on the walls. "*Ven conmigo,* he's in here. It's a wonder I didn't pray the hornets on him, *el pequeño alborotador,* he breaks my heart!"

Will followed with a purpose, and Lauren tagged after, cautious and unsure. She didn't want to get in the way, and she still had no idea what they were doing.

Rosa's small living room had been decked out for the holidays. A modest tree stood in one corner, trimmed with what appeared to be mostly homemade ornaments. There was no fireplace, so the stockings were hung from the entertainment center. Three handmade stockings, names painted on with glittery puffy paint. Her heart squeezed. She would've loved a stocking like that.

Lauren sat in the hard memories of her Christmases for a moment. After the divorce, her mother was a shell of herself. She stopped cleaning, stopped making lunches, just... stopped. It took her a long time to put herself back together, and because of that, Christmas became the loneliest day of the year. The first year, when they realized Santa had skipped right over them, she and Spencer wrapped up toys and board games they hadn't played with in a while, exchanging them and pretending they were brand new.

But by the third year, they were too tired to pretend.

Lauren scanned the tidy space and saw a kid—probably about eighteen or nineteen—propped on pillows, stretched out on the sofa. His foot was bandaged and elevated by a large cushion.

"Coach!" The kid's face lit up, but not with full excitement. Almost like catching someone eating your clearly marked food out of the office fridge. "What are you doing here?"

"Changed my plans so I could check in on you," Will said. "Wasn't sure a phone call was going to be enough."

"Nah, I'm good." The kid's eyes danced. He obviously didn't care that he was caught eating someone else's clearly marked food out of the office fridge. Lauren was reminded of a younger version of Will—charming, handsome, and from the looks of his attitude and his bandaged leg, never took much of anything too seriously.

Did those comparisons still ring true for her traveling companion?

The kid looked at Lauren, his lazy grin hanging lopsided like a crescent moon. "Coach, you've been holding out on us!" He smiled fully now, and Lauren imagined this kid was as dangerous to the opposite sex as Will Sinclair at the same age. "What are you doing with Coach, did you lose a bet or something?"

Lauren actually chuckled. *You don't know the half of it, kid.*

"I'm Jackson." He spread his hands out wide behind his head, relaxed. "Coach's star pitcher."

"More like Coach's star bench warmer. You know you can't play with that." Will nodded toward Jackson's foot.

"It's just bruised," he waved him off. "It'll heal before I'm even back from Christmas."

"Is that right?" Will took on a completely different demeanor. Jackson sat up straighter, now the pupil to the teacher. Will wasn't that flirtatious guy pushing all her buttons —he was the coach. And this kid was looking up at him like his opinion was the only one in the world that mattered.

Will sat on the armchair beside the couch. "Jackson. You know we need to talk about a few things, right?" Lauren watched a silent exchange between the two of them. Jackson's face fell.

"I know I let you down, Coach," he mumbled.

"You didn't just let me down, Pope." Will put a hand on Jackson's good leg. "You let your team down. You let yourself down." Then, over his shoulder to Rosa, "Not to mention the most beautiful woman in the world."

"*Oye, detente, hermoso!*" Rosa flapped a kitchen towel at Will, and then motioned for Lauren to follow her into the other room. As curious as she was, Lauren knew this conversation was private. As she was leaving, she overheard Will say, "Look, I don't tell you all this stuff for fun. You need to learn from my mistakes. You need to be better than me."

His mistakes. The words lingered, and Lauren couldn't help but wonder if she was one of them.

CHAPTER 10

"*Gracias* for letting Coach Will come." Rosa ushered Lauren into the small kitchen.

"Oh, of course," Lauren said. "It seems like it's important." Lauren felt the blush of shame rise to her cheeks. Will wasn't the type to explain himself, especially not about anything serious.

But this? This was a different side of him. One she didn't think existed.

"Rosa, do you mind me asking what happened to Jackson's foot?"

Rosa glanced at her, then bustled around her kitchen. She filled a tea kettle with water and set it on the stove to heat. She pulled a box of tea bags from the cupboard and some milk from the refrigerator. She was avoiding Lauren's eyes—and her question—and Lauren wished she could take it back.

"I'm sorry," Lauren looked down, then back at Rosa. "I didn't mean to pry."

Rosa turned to face her, and there were quiet tears in her eyes.

"I shouldn't have said anything," Lauren said.

"No, no," Rosa picked up one of Lauren's hands and patted it. "I'm just so worried about him." She looked back into the living room. "Jackson is a good boy. He has always been a good boy. But he didn't meet the best friends when he got to college. He does things now he never did before. Drinking, missing classes —he got fired from his work study job. He's on scholarship, and if he gets kicked off the team..."

"He loses it," Lauren finished.

Lauren glanced toward the kitchen door and into the living room where she saw Will, sitting on the chair next to Jackson, leaning toward him and gesturing in what appeared to be deep conversation. She couldn't see his face, but she could tell by his body language that Will was invested.

The kettle whistled, and Rosa turned to attend to it. "Coach Will." Rosa sighed. "Always looking out for my Jackson. Making sure he knows consequences. Making sure to use his talent, not take it for granted. Your Will is saving my boy. You're a very lucky woman." Rosa's smile was so genuine, it splintered something in Lauren's heart.

The older woman set a cup of tea on the table in front of Lauren.

"He's not my Will," Lauren admitted.

Rosa's face lit in surprise. "No! But you are both so beautiful!"

Lauren felt the blush rise to her cheeks. She shook her head. "We're just...well, I don't know what we are. Friends, I guess? I don't know him that well, he's just giving me a ride home for the holidays. He's friends with my brother, and we're from the same hometown." She thought she might shrink under the weight of Rosa's gaze. This stranger looked at her in a way most people didn't—in a way that allowed her to actually *see* Lauren.

And Lauren wasn't sure she wanted to be seen.

"I just assumed." Rosa glanced in the direction of the living room. "Any woman would be so lucky to have a man like Will."

Lauren gave a soft shrug. "I'm just not that lucky." Her voice hitched. The feelings she'd worked so hard to bury poked through her surface like a tiny bud shooting through concrete.

"Between you and me, Coach Will is a godsend. Jackson's father and I don't know where we went wrong with him, but he doesn't listen to us anymore."

"Rosa, sometimes kids just do stupid things," Lauren said with more authority than she had on the subject. "Sometimes the very best parents can't keep their kids from making bad decisions. It's all part of growing up."

Rosa nodded slowly. "Coach Will has said that too. He even gave me his mother's phone number, so I could talk to someone who's been through it."

Immediately, Lauren wondered about Will's real story. Not the story she'd assigned to him, but his real story. The one he only shared as a cautionary tale. After what had happened between them all those years ago, she thought she had him pegged. She heard what people said, after all. She knew about the girls, the partying, and she certainly knew that he had a way of making people fall in love with him.

Will didn't simply play the field, he left behind a trail of broken hearts. She'd always assumed he'd done that on purpose. Like it was a game.

Lauren took a few steps and stood in the kitchen, staring at him.

I'm not wrong. I'm not wrong about him.

She leaned on the doorway.

Am I?

"You like him, don't you?"

Oh, no.

Heat crawled up the back of her neck. Lauren squirmed past Rosa to the safety of her tea. "What? I don't. . . I don't really think about him in that way."

Rosa's expression told her she wasn't buying it, but thankfully she didn't say so.

A few moments later, Will walked in, his presence making her feel claustrophobic.

"Oh, Coach Will, *gracias*, you are a godsend." Rosa rushed over to him and threw her arms around his midsection. The top of her head barely reached Will's neck, and he hugged her back like he knew she needed it.

"I don't know if I made an impression on him. I can't tell if he's listening to me. I sure wouldn't have when I was his age," Will admitted, "but I'm not going to give up."

Rosa pulled back, wiping tears from her eyes.

Will's face softened. "If you and your husband can keep him home the rest of break, that would be good."

Rosa nodded. "We'll do our best."

Will glanced at Lauren. "You okay? Sorry for the detour. I just felt like I needed to come by. I don't know if it helped, but it was a chance worth taking."

Lauren saw something in Will's face she had never seen. Compassion. Honesty. Sincerity.

"Your *amor* and I are getting to know each other," Rosa winked. "And I think you two should stay for dinner."

Both Lauren and Will started overlapping protests at the same time.

"You're so kind, but we can't stay," Lauren said.

"Oh, we couldn't put you out," Will said. "Besides, we need to go. . ."

". . .get on the road. . ."

". . .find a hotel. . ."

Lauren and Will looked at each other, irritated that their lies didn't match.

Rosa raised her eyebrows. "Uh huh. *Veo como es*. Dinner it is."

"We can't impose," Will said. "And this one is pretty tired." He tossed a glance at Lauren.

"Okay, then I'll find you a hotel," she said. "Let me make some calls." She picked up her cell phone and walked off into the other room, leaving Lauren sitting there awkwardly, Will still standing in the doorway.

She should apologize. Here he was trying to do something meaningful.

"Is. . . he going to be okay?" she offered.

Will took Rosa's seat across from her at the table. "I hope so. Hard to tell." He sighed. "He's got more natural talent than any player I've ever coached."

Her eyes found his. "Is he as good as you were?"

His expression shifted, and for the first time, she wanted to know what he was thinking—what he was really thinking. Behind the charming façade he seemed intent on hiding behind.

"No," Will grinned. "He's *better*."

"He's important to you," Lauren said, realizing.

Will nodded.

"He's lucky to have someone who cares so much."

Will turned his head quickly and looked directly into Lauren's eyes. It was almost like he didn't know what to do with her kindness. He looked away, back toward the living room where Jackson dozed on the couch. "Let's just hope he listens to me. He's on a downward spiral, and we just need to set him on a different course."

"Do you need to stick around another day?" Lauren asked.

Will shook his head. "I couldn't do that to you."

"It's important." She fidgeted with the ring on her right hand. "I don't mind."

He smiled at her, and she gave him the slightest hint of a smirk. It was the first real moment between them maybe ever, and it sent a chill down her spine.

Red flags unfurled at the back of her mind, a reminder that she was in dangerous territory—a minefield for her heart.

And when Will said, "That would be amazing," it tickled

something awake inside of her—something dangerous and familiar. Something she did not want to go away.

"Well, I'm amazing," she said with a smile.

Am I. . .flirting?

He smiled and nodded his head slightly. "That you are."

The air between them charged, and she sat, held captive by his gaze.

Rosa returned before she could process his comment—thank God. If she had to sort it out in real time, she was going to be in big trouble.

"I found you a room!" Rosa said. "At a nice place in town. And you'll come for dinner tomorrow when Joe is home from work."

Both Lauren and Will slightly sat back in their chairs, unplugging from the previous electric moment.

"Great," Will said, absently. "Thanks for doing that."

A sudden fear struck Lauren. "You mean two rooms, right?"

Rosa's face fell, but not too far. "Sorry, they only have the one. I asked if they have any more and they said 'no.'" Lauren thought she saw just a twinge of a knowing smile at the corners of Rosa's mouth.

"I'd let you stay here," she continued, "but we have all the unwrapped Christmas presents in Jackson's room, since he's on the couch. Our house is just so small."

"We'll be fine." Will stood. Lauren stared at him, incredulous. "We will. We'll make it work. Thank you."

Lauren's heart pounded a drum in her chest. Sure, they'd be fine. Just fine. Totally.

Her.

Will.

In a hotel room overnight.

Together.

What could possibly go wrong?

Text Exchange between Lauren and Spencer

Sounds like you're getting the full Will Sinclair road trip experience. Are you having fun?

> If by "fun" you mean "spending every hour wanting to gouge my eyeballs out with a fork, then yes."

Has he broken out the Christmas carols?

> Good grief, yes.
> Does he know he's a truly terrible singer?

Yes. And he doesn't care.

> I've never met anyone who loved Christmas this much.

If we were in his family, we'd love it too.

> How depressing.
> Spence, you said he's different than he was back in high school. What did you mean?

<shrugging man emoji> He grew up.

> Like, for real? Because from what I remember, he was kind of a tool.

<laughing emoji> Not a tool anymore.

> How can you be sure?
> You know people don't change.

Maybe not, but they do grow up. Most of them anyway. Will's one of the best guys I know.
Don't give him too much of that Lauren Richmond grief, OK?

                                                  What's that supposed to mean?

That impossibly high standard you hold yourself to?
Nobody else can live up to that.
And before you argue with me, yes, you do try and hold people to it.
Lighten up a little and see if you can have some fun. You deserve it.

CHAPTER 11

❄

Will couldn't help but be amused by the look on Lauren's face when Rosa told her they only had one room.

He'd sleep on the floor, or the couch or in a chair, of course, but why spoil the fun? And more to the point, why did he enjoy poking at her so much?

They drove toward the hotel in their usual silence. Will was used to it by now, but he searched his mind for a way to draw her out. She must have questions; she'd overheard enough of his conversation with Jackson. Or maybe not. Maybe she really didn't care one bit about Will's life.

It was presumptuous for him to think she would. Or maybe he was just hoping for a chance to show her he had changed.

Though, to be honest—no amount of change would ever make Will Sinclair worthy of a girl like Lauren. He'd corrupted himself on too many levels to even hope she'd consider it.

Besides, how would he break that to Spencer? "Hey, man, I know you asked me to give your sister a ride home, but I sort of fell for her somewhere between California and New Mexico. You're cool with that, right?"

Not that he was thinking about it. Nope. Not at all. Spence's little sister, that's how he saw her.

I have two sisters. And I don't think about them as much as I think about her.

"So, which side of the bed do you want?" Will asked when they walked into the small hotel room. He flopped on the bed and stretched a model pose, head propped up, hand on his waist, rear end jutting out. "I tend to sprawl out. We might wake up spooning."

Her eyes flicked up to his. "Nice try. I don't think so. You'll have to sleep on the floor. Or better yet, in the car. The seats recline."

He should put her out of her misery and tell her where he actually planned to sleep, but watching her squirm was far too entertaining.

"Are you sure there isn't another room here?" She looked downright terrified.

He hopped off the bed and shrugged. "Rosa said no. I've never known her to lie."

"Maybe *I* should sleep in the car," she said. "I'm smaller than you, and it wasn't bad when we were driving." She started rolling her suitcase back toward the door.

"Wait, Lauren," he said. "Come back. You don't have to do that." Lauren slowly turned around. "Gosh, you're so easy to tease," Will chuckled.

Side-eye. "What's that supposed to mean?"

Another shrug. "It's fun to make you uncomfortable."

She frowned. "Fun?"

"Yeah. You get that exasperated look on your face."

She looked at him, mouth open, eyebrows up.

"Yeah that one. It's kind of cute."

She abruptly changed her reaction and narrowed her eyes. "And here I was *actually* thinking I'd misjudged you."

That was new. "Oh?"

She ignored him. "So, you'll take the floor, then?"

"I'll sleep on the loveseat," he said. He tossed the bed pillow onto it. "Honestly, it's really cool of you to take this detour in stride."

She looked away. "Yeah, thanks." She fidgeted. "I also just want to say...I was a jerk."

Will moved closer to her and put a hand on her shoulder. She held her breath and tensed at his touch. He lowered his voice to a soft, sincere tone, and tried to hide his smile. "It's okay...I'm used to it now."

She shoved him with both hands, laughing. "Ugh, you're the worst!"

He stumbled back onto the loveseat. "Admit it—you do have something against me." He was hoping, now that her defenses had powered down, that maybe they could clear the air. Spencer had never been one to hang Will's dirty laundry out on a line for everyone to see, but maybe he'd told Lauren. Maybe she knew everything.

Oh no. Maybe she knew everything.

And maybe she wasn't as understanding as her brother. How much did she know about his mistakes?

It seemed odd she'd take up this campaign against him if that was it. After all, his actions had only hurt himself. Not her.

Right?

She drew in a breath and met his eyes. He held her gaze for several seconds, hoping they could reach a truce. He didn't know why it was so important to him—despite Lauren's assumption, plenty of women didn't fall for his charms.

But Lauren was different. She was now and always had been *good*. Winning her approval, in a skewed way, could somehow make him good too.

A clean slate.

She abruptly broke eye contact and dragged her suitcase toward the bathroom. "I'm going to get ready for bed."

She closed the door, leaving him sitting in the small hotel room alone.

That truce would apparently have to wait.

∼

What is even happening? How did I get here?

Lauren stared at her reflection in the hotel bathroom's mirror, willing it to come to life and give her some kind of answer. How did she end up in a *hotel room* with Will Sinclair? How was she going to survive?

She scrubbed her face clean, dried it, and surveyed the hair situation. It was a mess after dozing off in the car. She pulled the elastic free and the messy brown waves fell past her shoulders.

She fluffed it with her hands, trying to add a bit of volume, turned her head to the side, and wait. . .what was she doing?!

Oh, for the love, Lauren, knock it off!

She was thinking about the way she looked because Will was on the other side of the bathroom door.

She threw her hair back up in a messy bun and ventured back out into the main part of the room.

"Care if I shower?" he asked.

Her heart sputtered. "Uh, no."

"I think the hotel actually has room service. We should order dinner. I'll buy since you wouldn't be here if it wasn't for me."

As much as she didn't want to admit it, he was being really, really nice to her. And she really, really didn't know how to handle it.

"Do you mind ordering me a pizza if they have it? Cheese and pepperoni."

She nodded, not trusting her voice. Something about knowing he was about to shower in the very next room had her insides reeling. And it's not like hotel bathrooms were exactly soundproof. Every noise would conjure up an image of Will. The water turning on. His hand under the stream to test the temperature. His shirt hitting the floor.

For some reason, a picture of the two of them standing in front of a half-fogged bathroom mirror flashes in her mind. Imaginary Will flexes, posing in the mirror. She shoves him, toothbrush hanging out of her mouth. They smile. Something that couples who have been together forever do.

Lauren Richmond, I swear, STOP IT.

He disappeared into the bathroom, and she ordered food, then figured she had a few minutes to herself. She pulled out her phone and dialed Maddie.

After half a ring, Maddie answered. "Girl! It's about time, I've been dying over here! Did you hook up with Cap yet?"

"Maddie!" Lauren hissed. "This is really, really bad."

"What's wrong?" Maddie's teasing tone changed.

She put Maddie on speaker and paced the length of the room. "I am stuck in a hotel room for the night. With Will. Alone. *In a hotel room.* We made a detour to see a player of his—an injured kid with a lot of issues, and Will was. . .well, he was actually really sweet and good with him. Even the kid's mom was talking about him like he was a saint or something. I mean, he's no saint, Maddie. I know this from personal experience, but watching him with Jackson, the way he so obviously cared what happened to him—I don't know, it was different. Different than the picture I had in my head anyway. But now, we're stuck here, in this tiny hotel room with *one bed*, and he said he'd sleep on the love seat, but he's still in the room, you know? *In my room.* Feet away from where I'm sleeping, and right now he's taking a *shower,* and I daydreamed that I shoved him and the mirror is all fogged and I don't know what to do!"

A pause.

"Maddie!?"

"Calm down, you spaz. I'm still waiting for you to tell me what the problem is."

"Maddie, I am trying really hard to hate this man," Lauren whispered.

"Why?"

"Because he is a recipe for disaster. A literal recipe. Two cups of charm, three ounces of inappropriate flirting, and a dash of dimples make for a very, very broken heart." She knew this from experience. Did she really want to put herself in that situation again?

Why wasn't her heart (or her pulse) getting the message?

"You're overreacting," Maddie said dryly.

"I promise you I'm not."

"You're doing the rambling thing you do when you're nervous," Maddie said. "And when you're trying to talk yourself into something."

Lauren thought about the fact that Will had changed his entire schedule, which whether he admitted it or not, was pretty important to him, just to connect with one of his players. To make sure he was okay. She was lying to herself about what a horrible person he was because admitting it messed with her resolve.

"Oh, no. Maddie. I think. . .I think he's actually a really good guy," she conceded with a sigh.

"You say that like it's a bad thing!"

"It is," she said. "Believe me it is. You just. . .you just don't know everything."

It embarrassed her to think of how horribly she'd reacted to what had happened between them all those years ago. How long it took her to recover. It wasn't something she talked about— ever. Not even with Maddie. Lauren had eventually moved on. Put it in her rearview mirror and forgot about it. Forgot about him.

Until now.

Because it was hard to forget someone who was standing right in front of you.

"Being stuck in a hotel room with a guy who looks like a superhero and who happens to be a really decent guy," Maddie said wryly. "Yeah, that sucks."

The sound of the bathroom door behind her caught her attention and when she turned around, she saw Will standing half in and half out of the bathroom in a towel.

Her jaw went slack at the sight of his abs, and she whipped her head away as if he were totally naked. Unfortunately, it was as if she accidentally stared right at the sun, because that image was burned in her eyes.

"Sorry." He sounded embarrassed. "Forgot my clothes. Could you hand me that bag on the chair?"

Lauren quickly took Maddie off speaker just as her best friend hissed a low "Oh my gosh. . ." into her ear.

Was he aware of the effect of his dripping wet body on her pulse?

Lauren continued averting her eyes as she walked over to the chair, then backwards toward the bathroom, holding the bag out in his general direction.

He grabbed the clothes from her, but she didn't turn around. "I'll change in here so you can keep talking about me."

She spun around to find him mostly hidden behind the door. He grinned. "Say hi to Maddie for me."

Lauren's cheeks flushed. Hard. This was a nightmare.

How much had he heard?

Had she been so wrapped up in lamenting her changing feelings that she hadn't heard the shower turn off? Or did Will just have superhero hearing that matched his superhero abs?

She groaned.

"I. Am. So. Jealous." Maddie said.

"And I. Am. In So. Much. Trouble." Lauren replied.

CHAPTER 12

❄

ROAD TRIP—DAY THREE

Over breakfast the next morning, Lauren drank twice as much coffee twice as fast as usual.

She'd spent most of the night staring at the ceiling, holding her breath, listening to Will sleep. He, of course, fell asleep in about ten minutes.

His breathing fell into a predictable rhythm, and still, it did nothing to lull her to sleep. Instead, she found herself replaying the events of the evening, wondering about his relationship with his players, wondering if he was as wonderful as Rosa said.

Jackson's sweet mom had recommended this little restaurant for breakfast, assuring them its modest décor was deceiving. "The food is the best in town!" she'd told them.

The sign above the door simply read "Café," which Lauren supposed was about the most straightforward marketing she had ever seen.

Like the rest of the town, the café had been decked out in Christmas decorations. Gaudy tinsel hung from the ceiling in swaths, creating a sparkly overhang, and there were signs taped to the window and the back wall advertising the many, many holiday events in El Muérdago.

Their waitress, a heavy-set woman whose thick, smudged eyeliner seemed to suggest she was wearing last night's makeup, sported elf ears and a little piece of greenery pinned underneath her name tag, which said *Dot*.

"You two just passing through?" she asked after she took their order.

"We are," Will grinned. "Thought we'd spend the day seeing the sights."

There were sights?

"Oh, you should!" Dot gushed. She ran through a list of Christmas events happening in El Muérdago, and Will listened to her like she was the most interesting person in the world.

Lauren noticed that he was every bit as charming and attentive to this woman as he had been with the young, pretty waitress he'd flirted with at their first stop, and it occurred to her that maybe this wasn't flirting to him at all. Maybe he genuinely enjoyed talking to people.

She was having trouble reconciling this revelation, which seemed to be something of a pattern.

"You *have* to go to the torchlight parade tonight," Dot said. "That's one event I never, ever miss. I take my Logan every year. He's nine now, and he loves it even more than the festival and the concerts. There's just something about it."

"What's a torchlight parade?" Lauren asked dumbly.

Dot's eyes widened with all the surprise of a woman who couldn't believe the question had been asked. "You've *never been to a torchlight parade?*"

Lauren shook her head.

"Lauren doesn't really *do* Christmas," Will balled up his straw wrapper and tossed it on the table. "She's the cutest little Scrooge El Muérdago will ever see." He winked at her, and despite the playful insult, Lauren found herself working to conceal a smile.

Dot laughed. "I can't describe it. Couldn't possibly do it

justice. You're just going to have to come see it for yourself. Be right back with your drinks."

After she left, Will gave Lauren a once-over. "You look tired."

"Gee, thanks," she said.

"No, I just mean—" he paused. "Yeah, I just mean you look tired."

She laughed. "I am tired. I don't sleep well when I travel."

Or when there's a hot guy in my room.

"Didn't get your full four hours, huh?" His lopsided smile was like a warm dose of sunshine.

She silently chastised herself for thinking so, forcing herself to become engrossed in the tinsel hanging overhead.

Dot appeared with coffee, or as Lauren called it "nectar of the gods."

She took a sip, savoring the hot, slightly bitter goodness. She closed her eyes as the liquid traveled down her throat all the way to her empty stomach. "Mmmm."

"Ooh, that's a good sign, Dot," he said. "You're getting a big tip."

The older woman giggled and walked away. Lauren shook her head. "You're shameless."

He sipped his coffee. "Am I?"

"I'm almost offended," she said. "I mean, you've flirted with every woman we've encountered on this trip except me. Even Rosa, who fell for it hook, line, and sinker."

Surprise skittered across his face. "Do you want me to flirt with you?"

Her face flushed. "No! I mean, of course not. I don't want. . .I'm just saying." She retreated back to her coffee, hoping it would help shut her mouth.

He took a drink. "Good. Because I can't flirt with you."

She rolled her eyes. "I know, because I'm 'Spencer's little sister.'" She said that last part as if it were a demeaning title.

And not your type. Too plain. Too bookish. Too nerdy.

"No," he said. "Because flirting doesn't really mean anything." He paused and then added, "And because your Spencer's sister."

Her laugh was so soft, he probably missed it. "I mean, it kind of does." She paused. "Mean something. You know, flirting. It means a lot more to people who don't experience it often, that's for sure."

She had his full attention now, and she felt a little too raw to enjoy it. She wished she could find a way to change the subject, but her mind had gone blank.

"I get that," he said. "But for me it's just a conversation and a few extra smiles. I like people."

"You like *women*," she corrected, but even as she said it, she thought of injured Jackson Pope and his mom. She wasn't being fair.

He looked away.

"Sorry," she said. "That's not accurate."

The hopeful look on his face when he met her eyes turned her insides out. Did Will actually care what she thought of him? He held her gaze so long she felt the red flag unfurl again.

"Well, at any rate, I can't flirt with you," he said. "Because there's nothing casual about you."

"What does that mean?" She resisted the impulse to tell him she only dated casually because that was the safest thing. She was a little too eager to prove him wrong—why? So he'd agree to flirt with her? Good grief, she really needed to pull it together.

He didn't need to know that the guys she'd dated were the ones she was sure to never fall in love with. The ones who could never break her heart. It wasn't his business, and he undoubtedly didn't care anyway.

"Please, Lauren," Will said. "You know you're not the kind of girl you date."

"Ouch."

He leveled her gaze. "You're the kind of girl you marry."

She nearly choked on her coffee.

He'd said it so simply, like it was obvious, like it was the only thing that made sense. But he had no idea what those words did to her.

"You didn't date a lot in high school, right?" he asked.

Her mind flashed back to her never-ending crush on the boy who had turned into the man sitting across from her. She shook her head, hoping he couldn't read her mind, trying desperately not to be humiliated by this little trip down memory lane.

"Why do you think that is?"

She scoffed. "Because I was a loser?"

He frowned. "Because you were too good for the guys in high school and they knew it. You were completely out of their league."

"Ha, right."

"Lauren, nobody was going to date a girl like you when all they wanted was one thing. And they all knew you weren't about that one thing."

"Oh my gosh, you sound exactly like Spencer." How many times had her older brother said the same thing? And why did the words mean more coming from Will?

"The guys also knew if they messed with you, your brother and I would kill 'em."

"Wait, what?"

He grinned at her just as Dot set their plates on the table. After she'd gone, he put so much syrup on his pancakes it made her teeth hurt. Next, he shoveled a bite into his mouth and finally, his eyes made it to hers.

"Come on, Lo, you didn't really think we were going to send you to high school without firing a warning shot, did you?"

"So, you're saying the reason I went to prom *with my cousin* was because of you and Spencer?"

He laughed. "Well. . .not *directly*, but. . ."

"And he was *shorter* than me!" she cut him off with a groan. "The photos were horrendous. I look like an Amazon woman."

"Hey, Wonder Woman is an Amazon Woman," he said. "Just saying."

"Whatever. Her costume is totally impractical for fighting."

Will paused, lost in thought for a moment.

"And if you're trying to picture me in that skimpy outfit you can stop."

Will shook his head slightly back, hands up in surrender. "What? No, I wasn't even thinking. . ." He paused again—"But now it's the only thing I *can* think of, so. . ."

She rolled her eyes. "Men."

"Hey, you're the one who brought the outfit up. I was merely admiring her for her fighting skills."

"That is the biggest lie in the history of ever." She buttered her toast. "And besides, I could wear a bikini to the Met Gala and I still wouldn't be the kind of girl guys go for."

"Because you're intimidating." He spoke around a mouthful of food, waving his fork in her general direction.

She laughed. "Because I'm...what? Ha! Hardly."

He narrowed his gaze at her for a full three-count, then she finally made a face and looked away, unable to make sense of this conversation.

"Now, what are we going to do about your lack of Christmas cheer, Miss Scrooge?" He dragged a forkful of pancakes through the syrup and shoved another big bite in his mouth.

"I'm fine."

"You literally hate Christmas," he said. "That's the opposite of fine. We need to fix that. It's a moral imperative. And," he gestured toward the window, "this seems like the perfect little town to do it."

"Why do you care if I hate Christmas?" she asked. "It's not like this is a new development. I've been hating Christmas my entire adult life and part of my childhood, and it never mattered before."

He shrugged. "I don't know, maybe because in my house, Christmas is a huge deal. Nobody decorates like my mom, and she goes all out on the homemade treats. She and my sisters spend whole weekends baking cookies and homemade cinnamon rolls. It's the one time of year we're all still together, no matter what. I think everyone should have that."

She looked away. "Well, unfortunately, everyone doesn't."

"I know." Those two words were so genuine they nearly undid her. Unexpected tears sprang to her eyes, and she blinked to keep them where they belonged.

Dot appeared at the end of their table again, that silly smile plastered on her face. "You two are just the cutest couple I have ever seen come through that door."

Lauren started to respond, but Will cut her off with a charming little, "Why thank you, Dot, that sure is kind of you to say." He flashed Lauren an amused smile.

The waitress rested a hand on Will's shoulder and for a split second, Lauren was jealous. It was such an odd, knee-jerk emotion. She wanted that ease. She wanted that familiar touch with him. But this strong urge to know Will that well clashed with the equally strong urge to push him away.

Part of her wanted to never be hurt again, but part of her didn't really care.

This crazy mix of emotions tumbling around inside her heart left her so out of sorts, there was no way to avoid being awkward while she processed it.

"You know, I don't do this for every couple, but—" Dot fiddled with her nametag, and for a second, Lauren wondered if she was going to take it off and give it to Will as a memento. But it wasn't the thin piece of plastic she was after, it was the little sprig of greenery behind it.

"You know what El Muérdago means, don't you?" Dot asked with a knowing smile.

Lauren and Will snapped their heads at one another (*Will holding in a laugh and Lauren with abject horror*) as Dot held the little plant above their heads. "It means 'mistletoe.'"

Oh no oh no oh no oh no.

Lauren felt the blood drain from her cheeks. Her eyes begged Will not to do this. Will's eyes, however, remained playful and dancing and dared her not to run away.

"Oh, no, Dot, that's okay—" Lauren laughed nervously. "He just ate a bunch of syrup, and it's super sticky, and it wouldn't make for a great. . .I mean, not that I don't like syrup or anything, it's just. . ." She trailed off, mumbling words even she didn't understand.

"You know what, Dot." Will placed one hand on the woman's arm. "On any other day, with any other woman—" he glanced at Lauren, "—I would be all for it."

Lauren's heart sank, but she didn't know exactly why. She didn't want this, but hearing him say he didn't want it either hurt. How much more of a loser could she be? Even now—years out of high school, moderately successful with a corrected overbite and contact lenses, she wasn't anywhere close to turning his head.

But I don't want to turn his head.

Right?

"Dot, the truth is, we aren't a couple."

Dot gasped, and brought her hand to her chest. "No!"

"It's true," he continued. Will then reached across the table and took Lauren's hand. "But if the stars align and things work out, the first time I kiss this woman is going to be because I want to—not because some tradition told me I had to."

Lauren froze in place, as if Will's hand on hers shocked her body rigid.

Dot let out a squeal. "Well, that was the most romantic thing I've ever heard!"

Lauren's throat went completely dry. Will's hand and gaze still rested on hers, a knowing smile on his face. Was it flirting? *Is this flirting? Is he just being nice?* Lauren, having a near out-of-body experience, couldn't tell.

She couldn't deny that a part of her was tipping over the precipice that held up her resolve. A part of her was falling for every single word, every crooked smile, every flash of his blue eyes. She *knew* better than to get sucked into this. She knew better than to give it any more weight than it deserved, which should be exactly zero.

Dot floated off, and Lauren slowly slid her hand out from under Will's.

"I hope that was okay," he said, as if dropping an act. "You looked a little uneasy."

"Mm hmm." She tried to stay calm, to put her insides back in their proper places. Her heart was suspiciously in her throat. Of course, he was only saying that because he knew the whole idea made her uncomfortable. Of course, that was it. Not because he meant it.

"I take it being put on the spot ranks right up there with not having an itinerary?" he asked.

She cleared her throat, forcing the words in her brain to stop mucking about and make a sentence. "Uh, yeah," she said. "It does, actually."

His face was all kinds of casual, as if what he'd said meant nothing. Probably because it *did* mean nothing. *'Flirting doesn't mean anything,'* wasn't that what he'd said just a few minutes earlier?

But then, he'd also said he couldn't flirt with Lauren.

If that wasn't flirting, then what the heck was it?

He was giving her an out—that was it. If she thought about

it, it was a kind thing to do. And thank God he wasn't legitimately flirting with her.

She should be glad of that...

So, why was the tiniest part of her disappointed?

She pulled out her credit card before he could grab the bill. "This one's on me."

"Oh, no way. I don't think so," he said.

"You got the last one," she said. "And besides, you really just saved me from some serious humiliation back there, so I owe you."

"Serious humiliation?" he countered. "Kissing me would be seriously humiliating?"

Looking slightly to one side, she half smiled and shrugged a reply—then looked up at him.

"Huh. Well. We can't have that, now, can we," he said, as if seeing some unspoken gauntlet being thrown down. "So. Bellies full, traditions avoided. . .why don't we go three for three and see if we can find some Christmas spirit?"

Lauren looked out the window and just across the street, hanging from a light post and waving gently in the breeze, was a Christmas flag.

A *red* Christmas flag.

CHAPTER 13

❄

*L*auren had noticed that when they'd left the hotel that morning, Will didn't check out.

They were now walking around this little town with a hotel key that was good for exactly one room.

"Okay," he said as they walked down the small town's main street whose Christmas decorations could rival Disney World's. "I have a plan."

"Please tell me it doesn't involve karaoke. Or ice skating. I'm terrible on ice skates."

"No promises."

Each lamppost was adorned with large Christmas themed decorations (*red flags everywhere*) that were lit, creating what she was sure would be a beautiful nighttime drive. The boutiques and stores along the street had painted windows with various wintry scenes, and Lauren was certain if she actually enjoyed this holiday, she'd probably never want to leave.

It was the quintessential Christmas town. Something straight out of a movie. In the distance, the mountains boasted fresh snow, and Lauren had to admit—it was a stunning sight.

Walking around the little town together, they almost seemed

like a couple. Or friends, at least. And maybe they were. Maybe that was enough.

"What's the plan?" She stuffed her hands in her pockets.

"It's a surprise," he said.

"I'll look for a large woman in a tent, then." She smirked, thinking of their first impromptu stop at Big Mom's Wigwams.

He laughed, and she loved it just a little.

An hour later, Lauren was standing at the top of a snow-covered mountain decked out in winter gear, dug from the bottoms of their suitcases, holding a circular inner tube she was supposed to use as a sled.

Surprise, Lauren.

She grew up in Illinois—she wasn't a stranger to sledding. She and her brother use to sled the hill at their favorite park all the time. It had been *years* since she'd gone, and she wasn't sure she had the right disposition to enjoy it or the athleticism to accomplish it.

She absently wondered if this Mistletoe Town had a hospital.

"It'll be fun!" Will beamed.

As Lauren watched the kids tearing down the hill at breakneck speed, worry crept up her spine.

"What's wrong?" he asked. "You look green."

"I don't sled. I mean, I haven't been since I was a kid, and even then, I always found a way to get hurt. Remember that one snow day we had when everyone went sledding at Kiddie Corral? And Benji Fritz came flying into me like a rocket? He knocked me into a tree, and I had to get stitches in my chin."

"How do I not remember that?"

She shrugged.

"So, this is like, revisiting a painful memory for you." She heard the tease in his tone.

"It wasn't funny!" She laughed, despite herself.

"Okay, how about we go down together? I promise I won't let you hit a tree." He sat down on the inner tube and patted the space in front of him. "This spot has your name written all over it."

She hesitated, weighing her options. With the line of kids behind her waiting for a turn, she didn't have much choice. Never mind that she and Will were the oldest people up there. Even the parents of these many rambunctious children were situated off to the side, watching, like respectable adults.

She sat gingerly, then pretended not to feel the heat of his breath on the back of her neck as she situated herself just so. Once she stopped moving, he wrapped his arms around her waist and leaned in closer, as if positioning her exactly in the spot she fit best. As if she'd been artistically designed to fit there, her back pressed to his chest, his arms holding her tight.

"This okay?"

She nodded. Her voice wasn't working at the moment.

He pulled her closer, and the warmth from his body radiated through their winter coats, heating her up from the inside out. "You ready?"

When she nodded, he inched them forward to the top of the hill, and they sat for a few seconds, teetering on the brink of pure, unadulterated exhilaration. And a question poked at her from the back of her mind—*Are you going to let go? Or are you going to remain completely closed off because you're afraid of smacking into a tree again?*

The irony of the metaphor didn't escape her.

They raced down the hill, side by side, and despite her best efforts to remain unaffected, Lauren couldn't help it—she laughed. She practically howled with delight. Skidding, spinning, hitting bumps that put air between her and the tube, they both finally tipped and collapsed in a heap at the bottom, her body almost directly on top of his.

She didn't notice the smell of his aftershave or his taut muscles underneath his winter coat. And she most certainly didn't pay one little bit of attention to the full lower lip that practically dared her not to kiss it.

She rolled to the side, still breathless with the sheer delight of their tear down the mountain.

They lay there, silent, looking up at the sky, then turned to one another for a split second... and immediately jumped up to do it again.

Their delighted shouts on the way down rivaled those of every child sharing that mountain, and Lauren finally decided to sell out to it, if only for the day.

For his part, Will seemed extra attentive to her expressions and her silences. He seemed perfectly in tune to what she wasn't saying. And when reality closed in, he turned up the fun.

It was, without question, one of the best days of her entire adult life. Because of him.

Who knew?

Her preconceptions were wavering. Her walls were cracking. She was—for better or worse, and she didn't know yet—changing her opinion about Will Sinclair.

When the tubing finally wore them out (it turned out they were no match for the kids on the mountain, who were still happily going strong), they packed up and walked toward the Jeep.

"You're smiling." Will's attentiveness unnerved her—left her feeling exposed and vulnerable. "I didn't even know you had teeth," he teased.

She hit him. "Ha, ha. That was actually really fun."

"Nothing like snow shooting up your pants to change your outlook on life." He bumped her shoulder with his. "See? Christmas isn't so bad."

She glanced up at him. "One could argue that tubing isn't a Christmas activity so much as a winter activity."

"One could." He feigned thoughtfulness. "But that would make one an argumentative Grinch."

She laughed. "I thought you said I was a Scrooge."

"Tomay-toh, tomah-toh."

They reached the SUV, and she stood on the passenger's side, waiting for him to unlock the door. "Hey, um. . ." She felt stupid and awkward. Why was this so hard? She cleared her throat, then called over the top of the vehicle. "Thanks, Will. It's been a long time since I had that much fun."

He caught her eyes through the windows as he hit the button that unlocked the car. He shouted, "WHAT WAS THAT? I CAN'T HEAR YOU THROUGH THE CAR."

She narrowed her eyes. "Very funny."

He hopped in and sat next to her. "Look, I'll be honest," he said. "I'm just glad to see you happy. It's not like this trip didn't start out. . .a little. . .not happy."

She didn't disagree. She was a Grade-A, first class, royal pain in the butt. A she-jerk in every sense of the made-up word. But Will seemed intent on living his life to do good for other people. Was Spencer right? Had he simply grown up? He *was* thirty now —a real adult with a real adult job. Maybe wisdom did come with age.

Her phone dinged in her pocket as he pulled out onto the road. It was a text from her boss.

Lauren, I'm attaching a photo of the artwork I'd like to use.
I know you're on vacation, but I need you to take care of this ASAP.
Can you have it overnighted?

Lauren's heart pounded in her chest as the photo loaded.

"Oh my gosh." She stared at the screen. "Oh my *gosh!*"

"What's wrong?" Will watched the road, his voice pitched with worry.

"It's from my boss," Lauren said. "She wants to use my artwork."

"Lauren, that's awesome!" His tone burst with pride and she could see he meant it. "Really, really exciting! Are you excited?"

She couldn't keep from smiling. She'd done it! This could be her big break. Her first step toward removing the "Assistant" before her title. "I really am. If she likes the designs I put together, I'm one step closer to become a set decorator on my own." She couldn't have torn the smile from her face if she tried.

She tapped a reply—

> Lisa, I won't have to overnight the artwork.
> I left it on my desk in an envelope marked "dorm room'"

You were pretty confident in this one, huh?
<winking emoji>

> I was hopeful *<fingers crossed emoji>*

I want to keep the artist's information on file—
I have a feeling we can use this style in a few other projects.
Send over whatever else you have from him/her!

> *<thumbs-up emoji>*
> I'll do it tonight!

Lauren knew she was beaming. For the first time in a while, she actually felt. . .*good*. Will flicked on his blinker and turned toward the Pope house, where they were headed for the evening. She glanced over at him.

Could this day get any better?

CHAPTER 14

When Will had agreed to give Spencer's sister a ride across the country, he'd done it as a favor to one of his oldest friends. But the air between he and Lauren had changed, and one thing was certain—he did not think of her as his little sister anymore.

Replacing the girl reading the book on the porch was this beautiful, closed-off, honest, waiting-to-be-cracked open woman who challenged his contentment simply by living her life.

He didn't want to be challenged. He was just fine with the status quo. Why did she have to go around inspiring him? It was not what he'd signed up for.

Worse, he couldn't stop thinking about her. He wanted to be around her. To make her smile. Heck, he'd make a whole career of that if she'd let him—and he knew it wouldn't be easy, which, honestly, made the idea even more alluring. She'd make him work for every single smirk.

He felt attracted to her that first day in the diner in Santa Monica, but that had been purely physical. And it had caught him off-guard. But what he was feeling now was more than that—and that scared him a little more than it should.

Watching her light up about this professional win had intrigued him. She put herself out there *so* easily. Much more at ease than she was with him, for sure. She saw something she wanted, and she had gone after it, regardless of how big or risky. He didn't do that. With women, of course, making people laugh was like breathing to him.

But career-wise? It just wasn't the case. It was too risky. What if he found out he wasn't any good? What if he lost baseball again?

There wasn't a day that went by where he didn't feel lucky to be where he was.

"You okay?"

It was the first time she'd initiated a conversation, and her question snapped him from his thought spiral. "Yeah, great!" He hoped the lie sounded convincing.

These weren't the kinds of things he dwelled on. Ever. He didn't have a five-year plan. He didn't even have a plan past driving down this particular road. But seeing how bold Lauren was with her career got him thinking.

Maybe. . .maybe I should.

The head coach position was opening at the end of this season. What if he threw his hat in the ring? What if he went for it? The worst that could happen was they'd turn him down, right?

He didn't deserve the job. Sure, he hoped he'd made an impact on his players and the team as a whole, but he'd taken baseball for granted, and part of him knew he needed to prove he was willing to work to keep it.

A voice nagged at the back of his mind. *Who's going to listen to you—the guy who threw away his chances at the Majors?* It was a familiar voice, one that sometimes rung a little too loudly in his mind.

But what if that voice was wrong? What if he took a shot?

"Worried about Jackson?"

Shamefully, he hadn't been thinking of Jackson at all.

Lauren's gaze was trained on him, and it unnerved him. She'd spent most of the trip so far avoiding his eyes.

"Yeah, I am. He's not on the greatest path." It was a path that Will had walked before.

He looked away. He wasn't the type to overanalyze his life.

Without even trying, she'd made him want more for himself. She was challenging him to quit settling. The sour taste of failure was still too bitter in his mouth to want to try again.

But maybe... maybe I should.

"Does Rosa remember we're coming? I need to prepare to be hugged again." Lauren gazed out her window at the small ranch home as Will parked the Jeep.

He turned off the engine. "She demanded it, remember? She made us dinner."

Lauren mused. "She really loves you."

She did. He only hoped he could have the kind of impact on Jackson that Rosa believed he could.

"I flirted my way into her heart." He grinned at her, having perfected the art of simultaneously acting totally fine while packing unwanted emotions in a box. He was desperate for the heaviness on his shoulders to lift.

"Let's go eat our weight in tacos." He wasn't about to let this heaviness follow him inside that house.

Joe and Rosa welcomed them into their home loudly, as if they were long-lost, beloved relatives they hadn't seen in years and not as two people who'd been there less than twenty-four hours ago.

"Coach!" Joe shook Will's hand and pulled him into a tight hug while Rosa wrapped her arms around Lauren. Rosa introduced Joe to Lauren, so naturally, he drew her into a fatherly bear hug. To her credit, she remained good-natured about the whole exchange.

Will inhaled a deep breath. "It smells amazing in here."

"A lot better than the diner food we've been eating." Lauren smiled.

"You are going to eat a home-cooked meal tonight! Entra, siéntate, tenemos mucha comida!"

Rosa hung their coats on a hook by the door and ushered everyone into the living room, where Jackson sat in the same spot he'd been in yesterday.

"Coach, they're gonna ruin Chipotle for you for the rest of your life," Jackson said.

"That's true, we are." Jackson's dad grinned. "But if anyone deserves Rosa's *authentic* tacos, Coach, it's you. And your beautiful girlfriend, of course."

"Oh, no, no, she's not his girlfriend," Rosa tutted.

"What? Why not?" Joe's eyes darted to Will. After sizing him up, he said, "She turned you down, eh?" Back to Lauren. "You're too smart to fall for this *bufón*, I bet."

Lauren's eyes found his, and to his surprise, she granted him a single smile. "I don't speak Spanish, but I know exactly what that word means," she laughed.

"Oh, Joe, leave them alone." Rosa stood at the doorway. "Dinner's ready, so let's eat."

Rosa had made a huge spread, far too much food. Homemade tortillas, street corn, Mexican red rice, carne asada and grilled chicken all made for—hands-down—the best taco he'd ever eaten.

Jackson was up and moving around, already much improved than when they'd first arrived.

Lauren sat quietly, but her demeanor had changed—softened, lightened—even since last night when they were here the first time. He held on to a foolish hope that he was winning her over.

Never mind that he had no idea what he would do if he did.

∼

After dessert—Joe's homemade pineapple upside down cake, Lauren helped Rosa clear the table, walking the dishes into the kitchen while Joe, Will and Jackson continued their conversation about baseball.

To Lauren, Rosa was an amazing wife, an overly concerned mother—and an even better cook. And while Lauren may never be any of those three, she appreciated it. Admired it.

This is what a family is supposed to be like. She shoved aside the hollowness that had carved a space in her belly.

Rosa filled the sink with water and soap and smiled over at Lauren. "You don't have to help me with this. You're our guest."

"I don't mind," Lauren said. "It sure beats talking about baseball."

Rosa laughed. "Coach Will hasn't given you his 'why baseball is the best sport on the planet' speech?"

Lauren's eyes widened in horror. "No, thank God, and I hope he never does."

Rosa was quiet for a long beat. She washed a plate and handed it to Lauren to dry. "Your Will is a really special man."

"He's not my Will, remember?" Lauren smiled over at her.

"Oh, right," Rosa said. "Though the two of you seem so *good* together."

As Lauren wiped her towel in circles on a wet dish, she replayed moments over the past several days. But Rosa didn't let her mind linger there.

"It means a lot that Will is so open with Jackson," the older woman said, pulling Lauren back to earth. "It can't be easy for him to watch one of his players repeating his own mistakes."

Lauren's ears perked up at this. Rosa was assuming Lauren knew more than she did.

"How so?" she asked lightly.

Rosa looked at her. "Coach doesn't want Jackson to lose his scholarship, to lose baseball, the way he did." She studied Lauren for a moment, then looked ashamed. "He never said this was a secret! *Ah! Dios mío*, should I not have said anything?"

"No, no," Lauren shook her head quickly as she took another wet dish from Rosa's dripping hands. "It's okay, Will and my brother are best friends. I know a lot about his history."

But not this chapter, apparently.

After that one fateful night during her freshman year of college, the night that split her young existence into 'before it happened' and 'after it happened,' she'd purposely distanced herself from anything having to do with Will Sinclair. It was surprisingly easy to stop tracking his every move once she'd made up her mind to do it.

After all, Lauren had distanced herself from her own family. She had a lot of practice.

"Oh good," Rosa sighed relief. "He said he took it so hard when he lost baseball. Did you know him then?"

Lauren glanced into the next room, where the men were engaged in some sort of wild debate about whether the Cubs were 'retooling' or 'rebuilding', and she nodded. "I've known him since I was eleven."

Rosa gasped. "And you haven't fallen in love with him yet?"

Lauren dried—then re-dried—the dish in her hand, avoiding the older woman's eyes.

"Oh," Rosa said quietly. "You have. Does he know?"

Lauren frowned. "Know what?"

"How you feel?"

"Felt," Lauren corrected. "I outgrew my crush on Will Sinclair a long time ago."

Rosa responded by raising her eyebrows and looking at her hands in the soapy water.

"I did," she said, desperately trying to convince both women in the room.

"Why?" Rosa asked. "Did something happen?"

Lauren did not want to be transported back to that night, nor the days following. It was a floodgate being held back by only a small piece of masking tape. She shrugged off both Rosa's question and her feelings and picked up a plate that had been drip-drying in the sink. "He broke my heart is all." She sighed. "And between you and me, I don't think he even remembers."

"Are you two solving the world's problems in here?" Will's voice yanked Lauren's attention to the doorway. Seeing him standing there while mired in the memory of his poor choices knocked her off-kilter.

What was she doing letting herself swoon and fawn and fall for this man all over again, as if they had no history? As if she was safe to put herself out there again?

This wasn't a trip down a snowy hill that might end with stitches in her chin. It was so much more than that.

"We are." Rosa teasingly flicked water from her soapy hands toward him. "And the Cubs are rebuilding. They wouldn't have traded *El Mago* if they were retooling."

"Rosa, you never cease to amaze me." Will wrapped an arm around the woman's shoulders and squeezed. "Now, if we can just convince your *husband*," he said this loud enough so the men in the other room could hear, "that his *wife* is RIGHT..."

"Don't listen to that woman!" Joe shouted from the other room.

Will laughed. "Who's ready for the torchlight parade?" His eyes fell on Lauren, and concern creased his forehead. "Lauren, you good?"

"Yep." She folded the dish towel, a fresh dose of her resolve firmly back in place. "Thank you for dinner, Rosa. It was so good."

"Anytime," Rosa said. Then she turned to her and directly

said, "You are welcome here anytime." She pulled Lauren into a tight hug and whispered in her ear, "I think he's changed a lot. Give him a chance to prove it."

When Lauren pulled from the woman's embrace, she found Rosa's eyes, encouraging and kind, trying to communicate an important truth.

Thanks Rosa... but you just don't know.

She didn't know the depth of Lauren's feelings all those years ago, or the way Will had humiliated her. They could be friends, maybe, but from this point on, no matter how many moments she montaged that Will seemed to be genuine and kind and good, none of those would—or should—change her feelings.

CHAPTER 15

As Lauren got into the SUV, she told herself to stop wondering about Will's past. She knew everything she needed to know, and there was no sense dredging it all back up.

But her curiosity wasn't listening.

After her freshman year at Berkeley, Lauren had stopped going home. She'd found summer work on campus and spent the holidays in the dorms, and later, in the off-campus house she shared with five other girls. She hated the holidays anyway, so it wasn't a big sacrifice, though Spencer had always made sure she knew he wasn't happy about it.

She'd forced herself to stop thinking about Will Sinclair—it wasn't hard after she saw his true colors.

Trying to do the same now—well, she wasn't nearly as successful.

His true colors, it seemed, were more than black and white.

If what Rosa said was true, he'd lost his scholarship, and, as a result, he'd lost baseball, the one thing that meant the most to him.

But he must've finished school, otherwise, he wouldn't be coaching.

What was the story? How had this managed to slip past her? And why didn't Spencer say anything?

Actually, why *would* Spencer say anything? It wasn't like he ever knew how she felt about Will. It wasn't like he knew—or could ever know—what had happened between them.

"You're deep in thought," Will said.

She bit back a groan. It wasn't enough that he occupied her thoughts, now he had to occupy her real life, too. She was doing a terrible job of putting him out of her mind.

"I was thinking about something Rosa said," she said quietly.

"About what?"

She hesitated. "About you."

He smiled at her. "Hopefully it was in Spanish, and you didn't understand it."

"I like her a lot."

"Or, maybe it was—how did it go—that I 'look like a superhero'?"

Lauren's cheeks reddened with embarrassment at the reminder that he'd overheard her conversation with Maddie earlier.

"Or was it that I'm a really decent guy?" He mockingly put a finger on his chin and tapped, professor-like.

How much did he hear? The whole thing?!

His thumbs rhythmically drummed a beat on the steering wheel as he kept his eyes on the road. They were heading to the address Joe had given them for the best possible viewing of this torchlight parade—a ski resort nestled right into the mountains.

"It's nice to know all the hard work in the gym is being admired." He comically made a muscle. His teasing tone almost made her rethink what she was about to say, but it wasn't in her nature to let anything go.

Why couldn't she just let it go?

"It was about your baseball scholarship."

Will fell silent.

Even in the waning light, she could see the color had drained from his face.

"I didn't know you'd lost your scholarship," she said. "Spencer never mentioned it."

His tone changed. His whole demeanor changed. "I asked him not to tell anybody."

"But, baseball was. . .Will, you were really good. Like, *really* good."

Will sighed and glanced sideways at Lauren. "Thanks. I. . ." He shook his head, stopping mid-sentence. "I thought maybe Spence had told you. I figured that's why you were so standoffish when we first started this trip. I can't imagine what you must think of me. I mean, school was always so important to you, and you always did everything right."

She frowned. She wouldn't lie and say she'd had nothing against him when she absolutely did, but she could honestly say it had nothing to do with his scholarship.

"What happened?" she asked.

He didn't answer.

"I mean, if you don't want to tell me, you don't have to. I was just curious."

Will looked at Lauren, as if deciding.

"Nosy. I'm being nosy. I'm sorry."

"*In. . .500 feet. . .turn left.*" The GPS had impeccable timing. Will turned into a neighborhood lit by Christmas lights. Lauren stared up ahead, waiting for the ski resort to come into view.

"No, it's fine," he finally said. "I mean, I don't go around publicizing it, but it's my past, and I can't change it. I only hope other people can learn from it."

Lauren sat, quiet and unmoving.

"Uh. . ." His nervous laugh told her he was flustered.

How often was Will flustered?

He drew in a breath. "I don't know how well you remember me from back then. We weren't really in the same social circle."

"That's an understatement," she said. "I went to prom with my cousin, remember?"

He laughed. "I think I relied on Spencer a lot more than I thought," he said. "He kept me out of trouble."

"He had to grow up a lot faster than he should've. He was the only adult in our house at the time." She tried not to dwell there. Anger reared every time she thought about her parents and the way they'd behaved. Because of them, Lauren and Spencer had a stunted childhood, cut off long before they were ready. It was like getting thrown into the deep end of the pool with no floaties.

Start paddling or sink, your choice, kids.

Maybe that's why sledding today had first scared, then exhilarated her. She'd missed out on those carefree kid days with no agenda and a singular purpose: *fun.*

"Well, I had two adults in my house," Will said. "And I was *still* a mess. I got away from the stability, and I don't know—I think maybe I was homesick and didn't want to admit it, and the first friends I made apart from my teammates were guys on my floor who were into some pretty heavy partying."

He pulled into a parking lot of the sprawling resort, bustling with activity as the locals and tourists alike prepared for what appeared to be a favorite event in El Muérdago. As much as Lauren wanted to know what a torchlight parade was, she wanted to know Will's story even more.

He drove the SUV around the lot until he found a space in the corner. He parked but didn't turn off the engine. Instead, he turned to face her.

"I'm really not proud of the guy I was back then." He didn't look away. "I was selfish and egotistical. I'd been heavily recruited by some of the best baseball programs in the country and ended up with a full ride at my top choice—a school that professional scouts paid a lot of attention to."

"I remember that. There was a big press conference, right?"

His signing day at that D1 university had garnered serious attention in Pleasant Valley. Lauren remembered watching it on TV and feeling simultaneously proud of him and heartbroken for herself. He was moving away—and she might not ever see him again.

"Yeah, it was surreal. I mean, I worked hard and felt I deserved it, but I also thought I was untouchable," he said. "When I got on campus, I treated people. . .pretty badly. Like they weren't important, or worse. . .like they were disposable. I skipped classes. I stayed out late every night. I was drunk more than I was sober. I started missing practices and tanking games and every time my coach would get on my case, I'd clean it up—but just enough to convince him I'd turned things around."

Even though there were bustling families, car doors opening and closing, and Christmas music echoing in the distance, everything faded from Lauren's senses—except for one thing.

There was only Will.

"By the time Christmas of my junior year rolled around, my coach was done. Just done. I failed a drug test. He called me into his office and told me they were revoking my scholarship." Will went still. Lauren could see he was both vulnerable and frustrated, his face drawn as he recounted the painful memory.

"I remember sitting there thinking about the way I'd acted, the person I'd become, and all at once it seemed so pointless. I begged him for one last chance, but he was adamant. He said, 'Will, I've given you one too many chances already. I'm not only doing this for the team—I'm doing this for you.'"

"You lost your scholarship, but you could still play, right? Just because you didn't have a full ride didn't mean—"

"I got kicked off the team. I haven't played since." He propped his folded hands on the steering wheel. "If I'd been injured or something, maybe I'd feel different, but knowing I am the reason I lost everything is its own kind of prison."

At that moment, she saw the pain in his eyes. Up until then, he'd remained detached telling the story, like he'd told it many times before, maybe even made his peace with it.

But for whatever reason, he'd decided to let her see how much his regret still haunted him.

In the quiet of the Jeep, Lauren's heart sank.

He'd lost baseball, and he had no one to blame but himself.

It must have broken his heart.

"Will. I'm so sorry. I had no idea."

He forced a disenchanted smile. "No one did," he said. "Except Spencer and my family. Turns out they don't hold press conferences when you screw up your life."

She sat for a moment. She hated what he did to her—but deep down she cared for Will. Not just in an attracted way, but *cared* for him.

"It's not ruined," she said. "Look what you're doing now. You're coaching. You're making a difference. And Jackson? You can't pretend like what you do doesn't matter."

"I know," he shrugged, "I know it's important. It wasn't my dream, though. I wanted more, I still do, but it's way too late for that now. Where I am is where I deserve to be." He stared out the window at the laughing passers-by.

He'd been punishing himself for years. And maybe she shouldn't sympathize with him—after all, it was his own choices that cost him his dreams. Some might argue he'd gotten what he deserved. But she couldn't help it. She wished she could take that pain and make it go away.

She supposed that's what grace was—a second chance that isn't deserved. Was there grace for Will too?

She willed herself to think of him as a friend—but a thought dawned on her. She began to put the timeline together. Christmas of his junior year was Christmas of her freshman year.

Christmas of his junior year was Christmas of my freshman year.

He was at the worst point in his life, and now she knew why.

"You don't understand, Lauren," he said. "You don't know how much my family sacrificed for me to play. It wasn't just a little hobby. I played year-round. They had to scrape together tournament fees and money for new uniforms and cleats. My sisters got dragged all over the state because my parents wouldn't leave them home alone, even when they were in high school, but they both told me it was worth it if—ha, not 'if,' never 'if'—*when* I made it to the Majors. That was always the plan." He chuckled to himself as he added, "I think Kayla had her heart set on me buying her a flashy sports car."

The joke eased some of the tension in the air.

"I let them down. I let them all down," he said. "I'll never forget my grandpa's face when he found out I got kicked off the team. It was the worst day of my life. I've never been so aware that I'd disappointed," he looked in her eyes, "someone I loved."

Lauren tried not to let those words twist around her heart, but she failed.

"He was the reason I started playing in the first place. He was dead set on me going pro. Did you know he played?"

Lauren shook her head.

"He did. Not professionally, but he was good." He laughed to himself. "He was the one who showed me how to throw a curve when I was twelve. Not the smartest idea, you could wreck a kid's arm, but he knew *so* much about the game. I loved that." He paused in that memory for a moment, but then his face scowled. "And I could've, you know? I could've made it. Everyone said it was just a matter of time."

His tone heated in anger. "But I threw it all away. What an idiot!"

Lauren didn't have the words to help. She wanted to. She wished she could.

"Your brother, man, he was the best kind of friend." Will seemed lost in a memory. "He came home from school that Christmas break and spoke hard truth to me. Said my life was my choice, and told me it was time to grow up. He drove me to a rehab program, then visited me every day until he had to go back for the next semester."

Lauren stilled. "He never said a word."

"Like I said, he's a good friend." Will glanced over at her, and it occurred to Lauren that this was their first meaningful conversation. Perhaps she shouldn't mark that in her mind, but she did.

"I think of how I'm coaching now, and I tell myself, 'that's good.' I've had so many second chances, I'm not willing to throw this one away because I want something more," he said. "I get to be around baseball—that's enough."

"But it's not, is it?"

His gaze followed a couple pushing a double stroller with two bundled up children inside. Their faces lit with excitement as they trudged through the snow toward the festivities, but she had a feeling he wasn't really looking at anything at all. "Between you and me—sometimes I don't want to be the assistant anymore. I want my own team. My own program. I think I'm good at this, you know?" The look on his face when he turned back toward her tugged like a weight on her heart. Like he wanted to believe it, but he was afraid to. She could only nod in response.

"But then I think it's kind of cocky to want more than I have when I don't deserve a second chance."

"I don't think that's true," she said.

"Nice of you to say, but come on."

She reached out and put her hand on his.

"Will. *I don't think that's true.*"

He looked at her hand, then up at her face. "You don't?" There was a brief hint of hopefulness in his eyes.

She pulled her hand back. "I think you found a way to go on. You changed."

Do I believe that?

"You figured out what was important to you, and, I don't know—not everyone can do that when life knocks them down."

He held her gaze for a long moment, and when his eyes drifted to her lips, she felt it in every nerve of her body.

The back of her mind shouted *Run away!* But she didn't. Instead, she sat there, staring at him, just like she had That Night.

"My boss is retiring at the end of this year."

Lauren pressed her lips together and squinted at him. "And why haven't you applied for the job?"

He shook his head. "What if they tell me I'm not ready or I'm not qualified or they don't want me?"

She didn't understand. She was so used to simply asking for what she wanted at her job. Deciding what it was and going for it—that was how it was done, right? She couldn't wrap her head around this contradiction in front of her. Will, so confident it almost read as cocky, and yet, nervous to take this risk.

All at once, Will shed his superhero costume and transformed into his very human alter ego.

"And what if they tell you that you're perfect for it?" she asked, quietly.

"My past has a way of not staying in the past."

"But you've proven you can do the job. Look at Jackson."

"That's not as big a deal as you think it is."

"Will, there are plenty of people coaching and teaching who don't care about the kids at all. Tell me I'm wrong."

He said nothing.

"You're not like that. You're different."

"But. . ."

"And I'm sure people would be willing to take that into consideration."

"Lauren, it's. . ."

"You should send them an email right now and let them know you want it."

"I don't deserve it!" he snapped.

And in that moment, she realized.

She found it easy to take risks in her career. She was confident, and she knew her strengths. She had no problem believing she could handle more responsibility—and that she'd be great at it.

But when it came to relationships, to putting herself out there with other people, she remained closed off, unwilling to risk getting hurt again. Very few people really knew her, and that was how she liked it.

For Will, it was the exact opposite. His magnetic personality drew people to him. He was easy-going and friendly and genuinely seemed to love getting to know everyone that came in his path.

But in his career, he held back.

We're both afraid of losing something.

Maybe they had more in common than she thought.

CHAPTER 16

*L*auren considered this for a long moment. Something in common with Will Sinclair—she never would've guessed.

She knew the Will from before, and was just starting to understand present-day Will. And, she figured, the best way to reach him was to rear back and throw as hard as she could.

"I think you need to suck it up."

He stared, looking a little dumbfounded. "Did you just say I need to 'suck it up'?"

"How long do you plan to sit in your self-inflicted purgatory?"

He frowned.

"You were good. . .no, you were *great*, Will. I hardly know anything about baseball and I knew fifteen years ago that you were great."

"Yeah, but—"

"You only get one shot, Sinclair." She pursed her lips and shrugged. "Might as well take it."

The look on Will's face was equal parts shocked and impressed. He opened his mouth to say something, then stopped and turned away. He looked at Lauren again, as if deciding to be convinced.

Will leaned toward the steering wheel. "Maybe you're right."

"I *am* right. So it's not what you thought it was going to be—that doesn't mean it can't still be something amazing."

She'd always believed in pursuing what she wanted, but she only now realized not everyone felt that way. Some people had legitimate concerns holding them back. But she believed in second chances.

I believe in second chances.

Or did she only believe in second chances when they didn't put her heart on the line?

I think he's changed a lot. Give him a chance to prove it. Rosa's words echoed in her mind.

He sat up straighter. "Okay."

The word stole her attention. "Okay…what?"

When he smiled, the edges of his eyes crinkled at the corners. "I can't believe I'm saying this, but I'm going to go for it."

"Then my work here is done." She smiled at him, but his face had gone serious.

"How do you do that?"

"Do what?"

"Just chase down what you want."

She tilted her head down, incredulous. "This from the person who can literally have any woman eating out of his hand after a hello and a smile."

Will shook his head ever so slightly.

"But I don't want any woman."

Lauren heard her own nerves in her laugh, and she hoped Will didn't notice the tremble in her voice. "What can I say? I'm impressive."

"You think you're joking, but it's true." He sat back in his seat. "I can't believe I didn't realize it before. You're amazing."

Stay cool, Lauren. He's just being nice.

The silence hung there, tormenting her, but her mind was blank. She searched for something—anything—to say. "So, this all happened Christmas of your junior year?" she blurted, quickly regretting it.

That's what you come up with? What in the world are you doing, Lauren?

He nodded. "Right before Christmas break."

She looked away. "That explains a lot."

Shut up, Lauren.

He frowned. "What do you mean?"

Her heart picked up pace, the way it often did when her mouth got ahead of her brain. She simultaneously wanted to ask him about That Night and never ask him about That Night.

Especially if he didn't remember it.

Is it possible he really doesn't remember?

Unlike Will, Lauren had decided a long time ago to stay away from alcohol for two reasons: 1. The calories, and 2. The taste. Not to mention the fact that Lauren Richmond did not like it when she wasn't in control. Alcohol made people do foolish things. She didn't want to be one of them.

However, her lack of experience in this area made it hard to know what to believe. She studied him for a moment, searching for anything that might indicate he wasn't being honest. When she found nothing, she said, "You really don't remember, do you?"

His shoulders dropped, only slightly, and he searched her eyes, seemingly desperate to understand what it was she wasn't saying. "Remember what?"

The hint of a memory played at the corners of her mind, but Lauren couldn't bring herself to relive the humiliation. She didn't have the emotional strength. Once opened, the floodgates of that Christmas would drown her.

She needed to let it go. She *had* let it go. It's not like it had affected her last decade. She'd moved on.

Why then, was this memory still so raw?

She steeled herself—and half-lied.

"I think you got really drunk at a party, and I drove you home. That's all," Lauren said.

His eyes flickered with something she prayed wasn't a memory. "I'm sorry you had to see me like that. I was a mess. Did I throw up in your car?"

If only.

She shook her head. "No. I got you home safe and sound."

His eyes darted back and forth, as if he were working to recall, "I. . .don't remember that at all. Did you, like, come into my house?"

She hitched her breath. "I got you to your door, and," she lied again. "You took care of the rest." She was not confronting this. Not now.

"Wow. I'm so sorry, Lauren. I don't remember that at all."

Thank goodness.

As soon as the relief washed over her, it was replaced by disappointment. He didn't remember. Any of it.

He turned and looked at her, sincere. "Thanks, Lo," he said. "You were a good friend even then."

She smiled and nodded.

Right. A good friend. And again, like before, I want to be so much more.

CHAPTER 17

Will hadn't intended to bear his soul—not to anyone, but especially not to Lauren.

He'd been carrying around his regrets like Atlas, desperately holding up the world, for too long. Somehow, telling her about it helped lighten the load.

She'd helped him. Again.

Then she'd asked that question—*you really don't remember, do you*—and his heart sank. His palms turned clammy, and horror welled up inside of him.

It wasn't the first time he'd heard that question.

You really don't remember running down Main Street in your boxers, do you?

You really don't remember stealing the trophy from Coach's office, do you?

You really don't remember passing out in centerfield that night we broke in to the stadium or your teammates carrying you home, do you?

But this was different. The look on Lauren's face told him so.

Oh, no. What did I do?

"We should get out there." Lauren's tone brightened the mood. "We don't want to miss it!"

"Right," he said dumbly. "Right." He was unable to shake the dread that had parked itself in his chest.

They got out of the car and followed the crowd of people to the open space at the bottom of a snowy mountain. Off to the side, twinkle lights outlined the resort buildings, and at the top of the hill, Will could see activity. Still, he had no idea what to expect. He'd never been to a torchlight parade, and despite the community excitement for it, nobody had explained exactly what it was. That made the anticipation all the greater.

He stood close enough to Lauren that their arms touched, and he had no intention of pulling away. She knew his secrets now, and so far, she wasn't running away. That counted for something, right?

"You know, I just told you basically my whole life story." He glanced down at her.

She met his eyes. "You did."

"And I still don't even know why you hate your birthday."

She looked away. "Nope. You don't."

Christmas music filled the air. A live band of five men wearing Santa hats and overalls was situated at the base of the mountain. Not too far away, a bonfire blazed, and beyond that, rows of small booths had been set up to face each other, a wide walkway between them, lights hung from one side to the other creating an illuminated tunnel. People milled through the space, buying hot chocolate and warm apple cider and roasting marshmallows in the large flames.

The band finished their rendition of "Rockin' Around the Christmas Tree," then directed everyone's attention to the mountain. A hush came over the crowd, and pairs of opposing streetlights flicked off, one at a time. The booth lights dimmed. Bright red flares glowed against the white snow as skiers moved into place.

"Ladies and Gentlemen," a booming voice crackled over the

loudspeaker, "Welcome to El Muérdago 's Annual. . .*Torchlight*. . .*Parade!*"

The crowd erupted in cheers, and Lauren looked at Will, mouth open with excitement, and smiled. For two Midwestern flat-landers, this was foreign tradition—but the excitement of those who knew what to expect was infectious.

In spite of the heaviness of their conversation in the parking lot, Lauren seemed to be enjoying herself. Regardless of her professed hatred of this—and every—holiday.

"Please, direct your attention to the top of Mount Tapa Blanca, where our expert ski instructors from the Tapa Blanca Ski School are getting into position."

Each skier carried a pole horizontally, and both ends had been lit with sparkling red flares that flickered as they moved into a line. Will thought there had to be at least fifty skiers up there. One by one, they traversed the mountain in large, slow, sweeping S-curves. The flares illuminated the bright white of the snow, like a stunning red comet with an endless tail behind it. He couldn't be sure, but he thought the skier's banks and curves down the mountain were timed to the Christmas symphony being piped through the speakers.

The crowd watched in quiet reverence as the skiers cut down the slope until finally, at the very top, a sleigh illuminated. In it, a bright red figure waved down to the people below.

The crowd cheered again, yelling and waving as kids called out "It's Santa!" in a cacophony of overlapping voices. The music swelled. Slowly, the torches that trailed down the hill fell into a line, pulling the Santa-filled sleigh behind them.

Will couldn't deny the unexpected tug of emotions that needled him, and when he looked at Lauren, he saw her wiping tears from her eyes.

He nudged her with his shoulder and leaned in closer. "You okay?"

She let out a nervous half-laugh-half-cry. "I think it's the most beautiful thing I've ever seen."

He wrapped an arm around her in a friendly side hug. "Miss Scrooge, I think we've finally located your Christmas spirit."

She sniffled and he squeezed her again before letting her go, but not before he noticed how perfect she felt tucked into his side.

She fit.

Once Santa reached the bottom of the mountain, the lights flickered back on and the sleigh slid to a halt. Parents released their children, who flocked to the sleigh, and though the show seemed over, a fireworks display was just beginning. Will and Lauren stood at the bottom of that mountain, ringing in the holiday season with a crowd of perfect strangers save each other—and it was a magical moment.

There was nowhere else Will would rather be.

They'd come a long way in just a few days. He and Lauren might actually become friends.

After the impressive fireworks finale, the voice on the speaker came on again. "Ladies and gentlemen, thank you all for celebrating the holidays with us! The Christmas market is still open, so peruse the booths, visit Santa, drink hot cocoa, and for those couples wanting to steal a kiss. . ."

Will caught Lauren's eyes, then pretended to see something else off in the distance as the announcer continued

". . .find the mistletoe hidden throughout the resort. Merry Christmas, El Muérdago!"

The buzzing crowd dispersed.

A moment of awkward uncertainty hung between them as they seemed to be the only two people standing still.

"Do you, uh, want to walk around a little?" he asked. "Or is a Christmas market too festive for you?"

The corner of her mouth turned up. He took it as a win.

"Sure, let's see if we can find some marshmallows to stuff in your mouth," she said, playfully. "Anything to shut you up."

Jokes. He'd take that as a win too.

They ambled toward the market, both slowing at the hot chocolate stand as if they instinctively knew it had to be their first stop.

They ordered, picked up their drinks, then continued to stroll underneath the awning of white lights hung overhead.

"I'm sorry about what happened," Lauren said quietly, avoiding his eyes and wrapping both hands around her cup. "With your scholarship and everything."

"It's okay," he said, matter-of-factly. "I deserved it. I can own my mistakes."

"That shows a lot of maturity," she said.

"Nah, I just learned how to take all of those feelings and push them *way* down," he joked.

She rolled her eyes. "*Such* a guy."

He glanced at her sideways. "It was painful for you to say that I'm mature out loud, wasn't it?"

She laughed. "I admit, I had you pegged for an overgrown frat boy."

"I get it," he said. "I think that's an accurate description of who I used to be." He stopped in front of a booth showcasing homemade jewelry. Pewter hand-stamped necklaces and earrings and bracelets on display. "But it's not who I am anymore."

She stilled.

"I drew my sister Nadia's name for Christmas." It was definitely time to change the subject. "Do you think she'd like something like this?" He picked up a necklace with the words *This Moment Matters* etched into it.

Lauren stared at it for much longer than he'd have expected. "Why this one?"

He shrugged. "I like what it says. Nadia's kind of like you. A little Type A, a little uptight." Lauren hit him, mocking annoyance. "Not a lot, but you know, she, like you, has a. . .ahem. . .a hard time having fun. Might be a good reminder to live in the moment, right?"

"I do *not* have a hard time having fun," she said. "I went sledding today, *thankyouverymuch*."

"Because I forced you," he said. "You're welcome."

"I would've gotten there eventually. And by the end, I was racing those little kids down that hill." She grinned. "And I *won*."

He studied her smile, noticing the way it turned up a little higher on one side, like she was holding back, and then it disappeared altogether.

"You said I don't take anything seriously," he said. "But really, I'm just trying not to take a single minute for granted."

She nodded her approval. "Then I think that's the perfect gift."

He winced. "Not too cheesy?"

"Not at all."

He got the attention of the young woman behind the table and purchased the necklace while Lauren meandered away, seemingly lost in the twinkling wonder of it all.

After he paid, he joined her at the next booth—a wide array of various homemade cheeses and jams on display—wondering —fearing—what it was that had her so quiet.

"Do you think I take moments for granted?" She moved on toward a booth filled with homemade soy candles.

"From the little bit I know about you," he offered, "maybe. But honestly, I admire your drive. I'm hoping some of it will rub off on me."

"Ha. Only if you're lucky."

He didn't disagree. Although maybe he had a different definition of 'lucky' than she did. "Soo. . .since you know my deepest, darkest secrets now, can we maybe call a truce?"

She stopped walking and faced him squarely. "Were we at war?"

"You were definitely at war with me," he said.

She looked away. "Sorry about that. I think…" she trailed off, "I guess I thought I knew you."

"Ah." He jabbed two thumbs at himself. "Frat boy."

She hesitated slightly. "Well, no. . .I mean, yeah, I guess. Just someone who loved sports and loved. . .girls."

Will pondered this. "You didn't like what you thought you knew."

She shrugged. "We're just very different people."

They walked a few steps in silence, until she quirked a brow up at him. "But even Elizabeth Bennet had to admit when she'd misjudged Mr. Darcy, so I suppose I can do the same." She stuck out her hand.

He felt his mouth crawl into a smile as he slipped his hand in hers and shook it slowly, noticing the way her cool skin felt against his. "No idea what you're talking about, but if it means we can be friends, great."

She straightened. "You don't know *Pride and Prejudice*?"

He grimaced. "Chick flick?"

"It's a book," she said flatly.

He shrugged, still holding on to her hand.

"It's the best romance novel ever written. Elizabeth Bennet and Mr. Darcy spend an agonizing amount of time misjudging each other and completely misunderstanding the other's motives. Their mutual disdain for each other is because they're both proud and prejudiced and. . ."

"Kind of sounds like you and me," he said.

Her forehead wrinkled. "No. Mr. Darcy was hopelessly in love with Elizabeth and. . ." She trailed off, a blush rising to her cheeks as he slowly raised his eyebrows at her.

"She falls hopelessly in love with him?"

She glanced at their hands, still clasped together, then quickly pulled hers away. "Well, of course. It's a romance novel."

"Right," he said. "Sounds kind of silly."

She gasped, then narrowed her eyes. "You athletes are all the same."

"Oh?"

"Have you even ever read a novel? Or is that too *boring* for you?"

"There you go, judging me again," he said.

She sighed.

"Just like Elizabeth Bennet," he said. "I know Darcy had his faults, but she writes him off pretty early on, don't you think? Makes all these assumptions about his actions and his personality, and all the poor guy is trying to do is take care of the people he loves. Plus, she was totally creeping in on his conversation when she was hiding behind the seats at the dance."

Again, she stopped, right in front of a wreath booth, a look of disbelief on her face.

"I might've misled you. . .a little," he said.

She raised a brow. "Just answer me one question—Jennifer Ehle or Kiera Knightly?"

"Kiera Knightly. Hands down," he said, to her astonishment. "And you and Elizabeth have a whole lot in common."

"Hey, look! You're under the mistletoe!"

Lauren spun in the direction of the voice to find a middle-school-aged girl pointing at them.

Will looked up, and Lauren followed his gaze. Sure enough, they were standing right underneath one of the many bunches of mistletoe hung around the market.

Lauren hurried away from it. "We'll have to be more careful where we stop."

Will glanced at the little girl, who shrugged and said, "Aww."

You and me both, kid.

He had made great strides with Lauren—they were friends

now, sort of. And he was lucky to call someone like her his friend, even if she was prickly. He kind of loved that.

It was more than enough.

He lifted his phone and snapped a photo of her, bathed in the dim white glow of the lights overhead. He glanced down at the image on his screen.

Who was he kidding? Being friends with her would never be enough.

CHAPTER 18

❄

Lauren lay in the quiet hotel room, the light from the lamppost outside the window barely filtering in through the drawn curtains. It was too dark to make anything out, but she didn't need to see Will to know he was there, laying on the loveseat, only a few yards away.

She could hear him breathing.

She stared at the ceiling, replaying the night in her mind on repeat. The conversation. The torchlight parade. The mistletoe.

His comments about her not living in the moment.

She'd judged him harshly, and it shamed her.

Their approaches to life were so different. Confident and apprehensive in exactly the opposite ways. He said she made him want to go after those things he never admitted he wanted—never thought he deserved. And she convinced him. Inspired him, even.

Can I learn the same from Will?

After all, he wasn't wrong about her—he wasn't wrong about her all those years ago either. Never mind that it was painful to think about, but Lauren wasn't the popular girl. She wasn't winning over guys with beauty. She was plain. Studious.

Boring.

Lauren's life, her history, her parents, her freshman year during Christmas break—she'd locked all those hard memories away in a mental box and figuratively swallowed the key. All that damage kept her relationally closed off and singularly focused, pursuing only things that had nothing to do with people. With the exception of Maddie, she didn't let anyone else in.

If she didn't, she couldn't get hurt.

But the problem she was starting to realize was how she had missed out on the moments of her life.

How does that quote go? 'Life is what's happening while you're busy making other plans'? That was absolutely Lauren. How much did she even remember about the years that had led her here? She'd been compacting her life into big projects and promotions —and that compacted 365 days into four or five events.

Time shrinks when it's not paid attention to.

She rushed purposefully toward her career goals, but what else did she really have?

"Will?" She whispered, her heart teetering, the same way she felt at the top of that hill with an inner tube in her hand. "Are you awake?"

"Yeah," he whispered back.

She paused. If she told him something about herself, she couldn't take it back. He'd know it forever.

She panicked. "How's. . .um, the loveseat? Over there?" Mental face-palm.

Will fake stretched with a loud groan, smacked his lips like he was half asleep, and said, "Oh, you know, can't complain."

Another pause in the dark.

"How's. . .um, the bed? Over there?"

Lauren did the same stretch and same mouth noises back at Will. "Good, good, I'm just living the dream."

A pause—then they both laughed.

The darkness made her brave. "My dad left on my birthday," she said quickly, ripping off the emotional band-aid.

Even without seeing him, she could tell he'd gone still. He didn't say anything, yet his silence only encouraged her to go on.

"I was turning twelve." She spoke to the darkness, a hotel confessional. "It was right after the summer you started hanging out with Spencer, actually."

"Ahh...I was such a punk," he said. "Wait. Didn't we steal your plastic horses?"

"Uh, *yeah*," she said. "You created an impressive war zone in our back yard with my horses as some kind of army."

"Cavalry," he corrected. Then, in an epic voice, *"And they turned the tide that day."*

"You're such a dork. It rained before I realized you used them, so when I found them, they were all covered in mud."

He laughed gently. "Sorry about that."

She rolled over and hugged one of the pillows to her chest. "I was deep in my horse phase."

"Okay, out of context, that sentence would sound really weird."

"It sounds weird to me saying it now," Lauren laughed. She found it way easier to talk to Will in the dark.

She took a deeper breath and held it for a moment before letting it out, the same way a bullfighter might before giving the signal to release a two-and-a-half-ton animal. She'd never talked about this time in her life out loud—not to anyone. Not even Maddie knew how deeply this birthday had affected her.

Lauren spoke. "My parents had been fighting for a long time by that point, and I knew other kids whose parents had gotten divorced, but I guess I never believed that would happen to us." She shifted in the warmth of the bed. "I woke up that morning, and I got everything ready for the party—it was in our backyard. Pony decorations everywhere. It was *quite* the sight, let me tell you."

She expected Will to make some joke, but he didn't.

"All my friends were coming. The only thing left to do was decorate and pick up the food. We were going to have stacks of pizzas from Joe's and a big white cake with white icing and a frosted horse on top. It was a special order, and we *never* got special orders. It wasn't like the ones you get at the grocery store where the person behind the counter writes your name on it in that gross gel frosting."

She paused, then added quietly, "I couldn't wait for that cake."

Her mind spun back to that day. She thought it was strange that her parents weren't there when she woke up, but she told herself it was fine. Maybe they were buying party favors or more likely, picking up her cake. They'd gotten all the decorations already. She could set up on her own. She hung the streamers and blew up the balloons, set up the food table and the gift table, and when she finished, she sat on the deck and surveyed the yard. It was perfect.

But when people started to arrive before her parents were home, Lauren began to panic. She was an independent kid, but she'd never hosted a party. Some of her friends' moms hung around when they realized her own mother was nowhere to be found.

Lauren took gifts to the gift table, arranging them neatly around the space she'd left for the cake. A half an hour went by, and her heart hadn't stopped racing for at least that long. Where were her parents?

She'd left messages on both their phones, but neither of them called her back.

One of the other mothers tried to take charge, organizing a few party games, and doing her best to keep Lauren's spirits up, but it was no use. Lauren understood what had happened.

Her parents had forgotten her birthday.

At the end of the two hours, her father's car pulled in the driveway, her mother close behind. At the sound of the garage door opening, Lauren rushed inside. Her dad stormed in, took one look at her and shook his head. "I'm sorry, kiddo. No matter what happens, you need to know, none of this is about you."

"What do you mean?" Lauren moved aside as he rushed past her, straight upstairs, where she'd find out later, he was packing a suitcase.

Her mother stormed through the back door and into the kitchen, took one look at her and said, "Where's your father?"

"Mom," Lauren wilted, "where's my cake?"

At that, her mother looked out the sliding glass door and into the backyard, full of people. She swore. "You've got to be kidding me. I can't deal with this today."

The guests had started to notice the commotion, and everyone had gone quiet at the sight of the absentee mother standing in the kitchen with the birthday girl.

Her father returned to the kitchen, holding a suitcase. "I'll call you and Spencer when I get settled, Lo."

"Dad, what are you doing? Are you leaving?"

His face fell, and he looked away, unable to hold her gaze. "I can't. . ." his voice trembled, "I'll call you."

And with that, he turned and walked away.

Her mom raced after him, slamming the door and screaming and swearing. Lauren crumbled into one of the kitchen chairs, numb. She watched, detached, as the other parents, hands on the backs of her childhood friends, ushering them out of the yard, whispering "don't look," and "just go."

Now, the heater in the hotel room clicked off, leaving behind a ringing silence. Lauren wiped her cheeks dry and flipped her pillow over to the dry side.

"Did you ever get your pony cake?"

Will broke the stillness, and she couldn't contain a laugh. Laughing through tears is an underrated emotion.

"No," she said. "No pony cake. Mom never picked it up." She was sad all over again at such a silly thing.

"So that's why you hate holidays," he said—a statement, not a question.

In a flash, she was laying on Will's bed at his house, after the party, whispering secrets in the dark.

She forced the unwanted memory out of her mind. "I guess so." She wiped her cheeks dry. "Nothing was ever the same after that. Our parents were forever on opposite sides of a civil war, and Spencer and I got caught in the crossfire. He started hanging out away from home more."

"Yeah, he never really went into the details of it, but he was over at our house. A lot."

She secretly wished she had done the same.

"I didn't have anyone," she confessed. "I spent a lot more time alone. I loved reading, and I know it sounds stupid, but the characters in the books I read became my best friends. The only ones who would never hurt me."

Silence in the dark.

After a moment, Will said, "You know your parents' issues had nothing to do with you, right?"

She scoffed. "I mean, I *guess* I know that."

"They were selfish," he said, matter-of-factly. "You didn't do anything wrong."

"I think we were just in the way." She sighed. "I got used to being by myself, so I stopped feeling bad about that."

"Do you think that's why you're always working?" he asked. "I mean, it's a sure-fire way to avoid opening up to people—staying busy with other things."

She drew in a deep breath. "Maybe. Or maybe I feel like it's the only thing I really have in my life, so why not throw everything into it?"

"The only thing?"

She laughed sadly. "Pretty much."

"No boyfriend?" he asked.

"Nope," she said. "I don't mind being alone." But the words didn't ring true. She added, quietly, "People just can't be trusted."

He was quiet for a few long seconds, and she wondered if maybe he'd fallen asleep. But then he said, in a silly superhero voice, "You know who *can* be trusted?" She could hear the smile in his voice. Leave it to Will to lighten the mood.

She winced, knowing this was going to be ridiculous. "Who?"

"KRIS KRINGLE!"

She groaned and threw a pillow at him.

He continued, unabashed. "Father Christmas! Papa Noel! The Plumper in the Jumper!"

"The what? You totally made that up just now."

"I did, but it's kind of catchy, right? I think we'll pay him a visit before we head out of town."

"You're nuts," she said.

"I'm going to restore your faith in humanity, Lauren Richmond, if it's the last thing I do."

She knew he couldn't single-handedly fix everything that was wrong with her outlook on life, but the tiniest sliver of her wanted to believe it.

"That's a tall order, Mr. Sinclair," she said.

"Eh, I'm always up for a challenge."

"Okay, well, are you up for the challenge of getting us home before the New Year?"

"Ooh, I hear that Type A control freak trying to rush me along," he said. "And I will remind you—I'm in no hurry."

And for the first time, she thought that maybe, in spite of her need to make and stick to a plan—she was in no hurry either.

She fell asleep with a smile on her face.

CHAPTER 19

ROAD TRIP DAY FOUR

Lauren woke the next morning, squinting in the light to find Will sitting at the small table beside the bed. There were two disposable cups of what she could only hope was coffee in front of him. She was instantly concerned that she had drooled or that her hair was matted to the side of her face.

"Morning, sunshine," he said, as she tried to covertly paw at her hair. "Got you some coffee."

"Praise the Lord." She reached for it, but he pulled it away.

"Not so fast," he said.

She groaned. "This is actual torture, you know that, right?"

"You have to sing your favorite Christmas carol to get it," he said.

"I need to. . .what? No, forget it." She covered her head with her pillow, trying to keep from smelling the sweet smell of heaven's nectar.

"Come on," he said. "Operation Restore Christmas spirit continues today."

"You know that acronym is ORC, right?"

"It's a work in progress. The finer details haven't been worked out yet."

She lifted the pillow and glared at him from underneath. "Using coffee against me is a low blow, Sinclair."

He shook the cup slowly, bringing it up to his nose in a comical whiff. "It's a *white* chocolate *mocha*."

She pushed herself up onto her elbows. "Where did you find that?"

"Coffee shop around the corner," he said. "I went out early to say goodbye to Jackson."

She found herself loving that he did that, and then hating that she was loving that he did that.

"You did?"

"Is that okay? I figured you'd want to get on the road right after we visit Santa."

"Okay, first, we are *not* visiting Santa."

Shrug. "Ok, but no gifts this year then."

"Don't care. And second, I *do* want to get on the road. We've been gone four days and we're still in New Mexico. But. . ."

"But. . .?"

"But I kind of wanted to say goodbye to Rosa," she said.

Mock horror splashed across his face. "Lauren Richmond, are you getting attached to another human being?"

She picked up another pillow and threw it at him. He dodged out of the way—and thankfully managed not to spill the coffee. "Can I have my coffee now?"

"You know what you have to do." He took a sip from the other cup. "Mmm. . . this is *so* good. Definitely the best coffee I've had on this trip."

Lauren weighed her options. He was her ride, so it wasn't like she had control over whether she got to stop for coffee at any point once they got on the highway. And the smell had successfully infiltrated her nose, wetting her taste buds with that flavor she'd grown to crave.

She was a caffeine addict, and she really didn't care.

She sat there for at least twenty seconds, glaring, trying to figure out a way to get the coffee without singing a stupid Christmas carol, but when she came up empty, she decided to dive in headfirst and call his bluff.

Lauren knelt up in the bed, took a breath and began to sing "White Christmas." Even though it was morning and she'd just woken up, her voice was clear and strong. She sang it as if she truly wished for every word of that song to be true.

In the middle of a hotel room, in front of a guy holding two cups of coffee, in a town whose name meant 'Mistletoe,' Lauren sang with an ease like she had been doing it all her life.

Will, for what she was sure was the first time in a long time, was speechless.

She nimbly got out of the bed, walked over to his frozen outstretched hand, and plucked the cup of coffee.

"Thanks," she quipped, owning the moment, sipping the beautifully warm, slightly bitter drink.

He shook his head as if to come to his senses. "That was. . ." he started, then stopped. "Is there anything you can't do?"

"I'll tell you what I *wouldn't* do—I wouldn't make someone do tricks for coffee when it's seven in the morning!" She scolded. "You're doing a terrible job of being my friend!"

He stood, facing her, only a few inches between them. He met her eyes.

"Who says I want to be 'just your friend?'"

A world of emotions rushed at her, and she took a step back. "Knock it off, Sinclair. Your charm doesn't work on me." She pushed past him into the bathroom and closed the door, heart pounding so loudly she wondered if he could hear it in the next room.

"Get it together, Lauren." She whispered to her reflection. "His charm doesn't work on you."

She didn't even believe it a little.

So, where did that leave her?

One step closer to another broken heart, she was afraid.

∼

Will made good on his promise.

She knew the instant they got back in the car they weren't headed out of town.

They were headed for Main Street.

They were headed for Santa.

Will parked in a lot across the street from what appeared to be an entire block that had been turned into Santa's Village. Lauren took one look at the long line filled with children—some of them crying, some of them hiding behind their mothers, one of them running around in circles pretending to shoot everyone else in the line (*for some reason she thought about Red Ryder Carbine Action BB guns*) and she shook her head.

"We are not doing this."

"I promise you we are." He flashed her that grin that was altogether too happy for this time of day and this particular circumstance, and then he got out of the car.

She groaned like a kid being dragged around shoe-shopping.

They took their spots at the back of the line, and a little girl looked up at them and said, "You're too old to visit Santa."

Will knelt, looked her square in the face and said, "You're never too old to visit Santa."

He was so earnest when he said it that the girl's mother swooned. Lauren was both jealous and comforted by the fact that she wasn't the only one who couldn't resist Will's charisma.

When they finally reached the front of the line, he gleefully stepped forward. The man in the Santa suit looked surprised. "Well, young man, you're a little older than most of the children I've seen. What can I do for you?"

"Not for me." Will ushered Lauren forward. "For my friend. She's lost her Christmas spirit."

"Is that right?" Santa *ho-ho-ho'd*, hands propped on his very real bowl full of jelly.

Lauren had to give the guy credit. His beard was real—not one of those cotton ones that hung over his ears—and he wore a pair of small circle glasses, which added to the overall Vintage Santa look.

St. Nick turned to the elves on either side of him, both with ears as pointy as their shoes. "Not the first case of Christmas spirit gone missing we've seen, is it?"

The elves chortled a response, nodding playfully at one another. Off to the side, Mrs. Claus handed out cookies to a little boy who'd just cried his way through the line. At the sight of her, the boy shrieked.

All in all, the place was a zoo, and thanks to Will, she was smack in the middle of it.

"Young lady, is this true?" Santa asked. "You've lost your Christmas spirit?"

Lauren forced herself not to roll her eyes. She glanced at Will, who wore a knowing expression that seemed to say *go in the corner and think about what you've done.*

"She's a little shy, Santa." Will gave her a patronizing nod.

"So, how can I help?" Santa's low voice boomed.

"I don't think you can," she said. "No offense."

"Nobody has more Christmas spirit than you, St. Nick," Will interjected.

Lauren shot him a silent *"would you shut up?"* and looked back at Santa with a forced smile. "I think I'm fine."

"Well, then, why don't you tell me what you want for Christmas?" he asked.

Lauren's eyes darted back to Will, who looked on like this was the most perfectly normal thing in the world—a grown woman, visiting Santa.

"Come on," Santa said. "You can whisper it if you don't want to say it out loud. I'm betting it's a little more complex than most of the wishes I've heard today."

Slowly, and only because she knew she wasn't going to get

out of it, she moved toward the man in the bright red suit. She leaned toward him, closed her eyes, and said quietly, "I want my pony birthday cake."

The wish was as ridiculous as the situation. Yet still, a part of her—infinitesimally small—thought there might be a chance she'd open her eyes and it would be sitting there, in Santa's hands.

He whispered quietly to her, "So, not so different from the other wishes after all." She leaned back as he smiled broadly. "Anything else?"

I want to love Christmas again, like I did when I had a real family.

"No," she said. "That's all."

"Very well," Santa said, as if he was a genie granting wishes to everyone who rubbed his lamp.

"Should we get a picture?" one of the elves raced forward and clapped her hands together far too excitedly.

"No, that's—"

"Definitely," Will interrupted. He jumped in on the opposite side of Santa and instantly cheesed for the camera, pointing at him with his mouth open like he couldn't believe he was getting a picture with the real Santa.

The elf snapped a couple of photos, then smiled brightly. "All right, off with you both to find Mrs. Claus and her tray of Christmas cookies." She spoke to them like they were the same age as everyone else in the line.

"Don't I get to tell Santa my wish?" Will frowned at the elf.

"Oh, of course, young man." Her tone reminded Lauren of a preschool teacher. "Go right ahead."

He shooed Lauren off with the bubbly little elf and took a seat right on the old man's lap. Santa grunted under the weight of him and the children at the front of the line pointed and giggled. Will leaned toward Santa, cupped a hand in front of his mouth and whispered into the old man's ear. Santa responded quietly and after a quick conversation, Will clapped him on the shoulder and stood.

"Have yourself a merry Christmas, Santa." Will gave a quick salute, then joined Lauren off to the side.

"Super-secret Santa business?"

He grinned. "I'll never tell."

They continued through the village and found Mrs. Claus, a plump, older woman who looked like the grandma in a Christmas movie. "Merry Christmas! Would you like a cookie?" She smiled as she held up a tray.

"These look incredible." Will reached over and took one. "Did you make these yourself or did you have one of the elves do it for you?"

The old woman laughed. "This is a family recipe."

He took a bite. "Mmm, it might be the best cookie I've ever had."

Lauren took a cookie and thanked Mrs. Claus, marveling at Will's joy. She tried to find fault with it, but it felt genuine. He seemed authentically happy to be in that exact place at that exact moment.

They walked over to a small prop house decorated on the outside with large cardboard candies in festive colors. Another elf stood behind a counter, clicking around on a computer.

"Ah-ha, there we go," the elf said. "Your photos are ready." He nodded down to an iPad.

"I don't care what they look like," Will said. "I'm buying them."

"I probably had my eyes closed." Lauren followed him over to the counter. "I usually do."

But she didn't have her eyes closed. She wasn't even looking at the camera. Instead, her eyes were fully open and entirely fixed on Will, a small smile and an undeniable look of admiration on her face. Her stomach bottomed out.

What the. . .?

"It's great!" Will cheerfully pointed. "You actually look like you don't hate me."

"I'm a good actor." But even she knew she wasn't fooling anyone. He was being kind choosing not to embarrass her because he absolutely could've teased her for weeks over this.

Will ordered two prints, and when they popped out of the printer, he handed one to her.

"A memento of that time you went on a cross-country Christmas road trip with your good old friend, Will Sinclair." He smiled, then added, "I think they have elf ears in the gift shop. Let's go get some."

She couldn't help it—she laughed. He was funny when he wasn't being annoying, and she was beginning to realize he was being annoying far less than he'd been at the start of this trip.

And that revelation scared her to death.

CHAPTER 20

Lauren warmed her hands on the heating vent of Will's Jeep. "If we're going to be friends, we have to compromise a little. I've put up with your serious lack of a plan, your detours, your stopping at every single old gas station—"

"*Vintage* gas station—" he interjected.

She ignored him. "—between here and LA. Maybe we could do a day that actually sticks to a schedule?"

Will tapped the steering wheel with his thumb and pretended to consider Lauren's request. "I don't know," he said, as if he was twelve, deciding whether or not to trade baseball cards with another kid. "That doesn't sound fun to me."

She rolled her eyes. "Everything doesn't have to be fun. Everything *isn't* fun."

"To you."

She sighed. "I want to get home before Helen has the baby. Can today be just about making really good time?"

If he had horn-rimmed glasses, he would've looked over them. "I'll consider it."

I won't consider it.

How could he when there was still so much to see?

Now that he and Lauren were friends, or at least friendly, the trip became far more enjoyable. A bit more like a vacation, though he wouldn't tell her so. He didn't want to rush through this, wherever it may lead.

Thankfully, she wasn't paying close enough attention to realize he wasn't taking the most direct route to Chicago. He wanted to get back to the historic highway he'd traveled all those years ago. Despite their new-found connection, he still didn't think he could explain why.

Not yet.

He placated her by *only* stopping at the most memorable spots—the giant road sign that let them know they were officially in Oklahoma, an old Art Deco styled Conoco station that looked like the real-life inspiration for the animated movie, *Cars*, and a quick drive through the historic downtown in Sayre, Oklahoma, where they indulged in ice cream at one of the country's oldest soda fountains.

He snapped several photos at each of location, chronicling even the smallest details of the trip, making every single moment into a memory. He also managed to take a few more candid ones of Lauren.

They took turns playing songs for each other on her Spotify, and he made her laugh more than once with his horrendously off-key singing. When that got old, she forced him to dictate to her a letter expressing interest in the head coaching position, which he still wasn't sure he wanted to send. And after that, she dozed off for a good hour while he concentrated on the sounds of the road and not on how adorable she looked lightly snoring in his passenger seat.

If he didn't count the beginning of the trip, Lauren actually made a pretty excellent travel companion.

In honor of her wish, he drove a little later than in previous days, but when the sun started to drop in the sky, he pulled off onto the shoulder, turned on his hazards, got out of the SUV and sat on the hood, taking in the scene before him. He wasn't the type to let a moment pass, not when the moment was this good. Up ahead was nothing but open plains—miles and miles of fields and farmland, and while he could appreciate the stellar views of oceans or snow-capped mountains rising over a horizon, there was something so familiar, so comforting, about this scene in front of him now.

Tonight, God was showing off, as pink and blue melded into purple, touched with a warm orange glow and the outline of the clouds, the fields, and the dusty road that seemed to stretch out in front of them forever.

The passenger side clicked open and Lauren got out of the Jeep, joining him on the hood. She said nothing, only fixed her gaze on the spectacular view in front of them, as if she knew the moment needed no words.

Then, just before the sun disappeared, she held her phone up and snapped a photo of him.

"For your scrapbook," she said.

He smiled. Man, he liked being around her. It surprised him, really, given how different they were and how little they had in common. He may have promised Spencer he'd keep his distance from her, but that seemed like a million years ago.

Before, the promise made sense. He wouldn't have been any good for Lauren, no matter how good she probably would've been for him. Thinking back on how he was, he shuddered. Sometimes flashes of his previous actions would paralyze him, and he had to literally shake them out of his head.

He couldn't change what was. His friendship with Lauren was new. It meant something to him.

Why then, did he reach over and tuck a strand of hair behind her ear? He wanted a better view of her face—but there was no way he was going to say that out loud.

She stiffened at his touch, and he quickly pulled his hand away.

What was I thinking?

This wasn't just some girl—this was Lauren. *Lauren, the girl you marry.*

She shifted. "It looks a little like home." The words sounded flat, even to him.

He should apologize or say something witty. But try as he might, he couldn't find words.

"Wanna know something crazy?" She slid off the hood to the side of the car. "When I'm in California, I miss the cornfields."

He watched her as she tucked her hands in her jeans' pockets, her face lit by the gentle glow of the sun slipping out of sight. "Oh, that's not so crazy."

"You don't think?" She faced him. "I mean, most people probably don't find Illinois to be very beautiful. We don't have mountains or oceans, but we have so much *green*. It's not green in California. I miss it sometimes."

"I get that," he said. "I miss it too."

Common ground.

She smiled, and he felt himself relax, hoping this meant she wasn't reading too much into his stupid move.

"If you miss it, maybe you should go back more often," he said.

She shrugged. "Besides Spencer, it's about the only thing I miss."

He hated that for her, but he didn't say so.

Once the sun was tucked in for the night, they got back in the car and drove toward the next town to find a place to stay.

"Don't you get lonely out in California over the holidays?"

She shrugged. "Not really. We keep it pretty low key. Maddie and I usually exchange white elephant gifts, eat pizza and watch *Die Hard*. At least that's what we used to do. She has a pretty serious boyfriend now—Dylan—and she's meeting his family for the first time this year, so she's spending the holidays in Portland."

He chuckled. "Did you say 'Die Hard?'"

"Best Christmas movie ever made." When Lauren glanced at him, her smile nearly knocked him over. It was different from her other smiles—brighter, less guarded. "We usually end up watching all of them, but the first one is by far my favorite. I love Alan Rickman. Do you know that was his first movie? He was a stage actor, I mean, of course he was with that voice, but *Die Hard* was his first time on the big screen. Crazy, right? He was forty-one."

"Wow. *Pride and Prejudice*. . .*Die Hard*." He held up a hand for each and weighed them invisibly.

"I'm an enigma."

He came to a stop in front of the first hotel he found, put the car in park and looked at her. "Yeah, you really are."

Her smile faded and the tension in the air thickened. He wanted to kiss her so badly. Lauren. Spencer's little sister—who was anything but a kid anymore.

"Lauren, I—"

"Let's hope this place has two rooms and no spiders." She opened her car door and rushed out before his big, fool mouth could ruin everything.

CHAPTER 21

❄

Text from Lauren to Maddie—12:36 AM

Maddie, this is a disaster.

No, a disaster is knowing that your boyfriend's mother hates you. . .

I'm sure she doesn't hate you. . .

Oh, no. She does.
Last night, they thought I'd gone to bed, but I was still in the kitchen looking for their liquor and I actually heard her say, "I don't like her, Dylan. She seems all wrong for you."

<gasping face emoji>
What did Dylan say?

He said she wasn't being fair—
That she didn't give me a chance.
In her defense, she did always picture him with someone who was more of an adult.

                                What do you mean? You're an adult.

Lo, I only own two plates.
I wear Mickey Mouse underwear.

                                Wait. Is his face in the front or the back?

<crying laughing face emoji>
I force Dylan to play hide-and-seek with me in the grocery store—
Not to mention I survive exclusively on Cheetos and frozen pizza. . .
I'm a literal child.

                                You're the best grown-up child I know!

<thumbs-up emoji>
Now, what disaster?

                                                    It's not important.

<wide eyed staring face emoji>

                                                    . . .

Don't make me call you.

                                                    Don't, I'm fine.

    Lauren's phone vibrated. She clicked it off.

                                        Cyber bullying is a crime.

    Lauren's phone vibrated again. She clicked it off—again.

                                                            FINE!

Good girl <heart emoji>

<cringe face> I think I like him.

<party hat emoji> <dancing lady emoji> <punching fist emoji>

No, Maddie.
This is bad. This is very, VERY bad.

What's so bad about it?

There are two people in the world who have broken my heart—
My dad and Will Sinclair.

<sad emoji>

I just can't. Not again. <sad face emoji>

But what if he doesn't break it?
What if he FIXES IT...?
And then he protects it like it was his most precious treasure *as long as you both shall live?*
<British guard emoji> <hammer emoji> <diamond ring emoji>

<eyeroll emoji>

You like him, right?
You never like anyone. . .
I give you permission to see where this goes. And if he does break your heart, I'll be there to pick up the pieces and glue it back together. . .
And kick his <peach emoji>

<Laughing emoji>
Thanks, Maddie *<heart emoji>*
Now go win Dylan's mom over with your undeniable charm. . .
And your great big heart.

It shall be done.

<heart emoji>

CHAPTER 22

❄

ROAD TRIP—DAY FIVE

The goal was to make it to Kansas, but ten miles from the state line, after a full day of driving, they blew a tire and nearly spun out on the highway.

While Lauren panicked and started looking up numbers for tow trucks in the area, Will hopped out like it was no big deal. In the side mirror, she watched him open the hatch and remove the spare tire along with a bunch of tools she didn't know the names of. Was he going to change the tire right here on the highway?

She exited the car. "It's getting late. Shouldn't we call a tow truck?"

"Nah," he said coolly. "I'll change the tire and we'll drive to the next town. See if we can get a new tire. They probably won't be able to do anything with it till tomorrow morning anyway."

She sighed. "At this rate, we're never going to get home."

"Oh, ye of little faith." He squinted up at her and winked. "You wanna learn how to change a tire?"

"What makes you think I don't already know?"

He stopped and looked at her. "Wait. Do you?"

"No, but you assumed I didn't."

He held out the wrench. "I'd happily move out of the way and let you take care of this."

She feigned insult. "Nope. You just assumed I couldn't because I'm a girl."

"That's not true," he said. Then, after the perfect pause for comedic timing, "I assumed you couldn't because you're a woman." He affixed the wrench to the lug nut and muscled it loose.

Lauren gasped. "That is totally sexist! You won't even let me drive the car." She folded her arms over her chest and stared him down.

He stopped cranking and conceded. "That's a good point."

"So, I can drive?"

He went back to cranking. "Absolutely not."

She groaned and shook her head, and he got back to work. About half an hour later, they were driving again. She had to admit, his competence in a crisis made him—(*grumble*) *sexy*—which was saying something given her attraction for him was already a seventeen out of ten.

He found a repair shop and dropped the car. Thankfully the store wasn't closed yet, and the owner could provide them a ride to a nearby hotel. Unlike most of the places they'd stayed so far on this trip, this hotel would best be described as "swanky." The lobby looked like a film set, decked out with crystal chandeliers, giant Christmas wreaths, a tall, perfectly decorated tree and white twinkle lights that made their entrance feel dramatic.

"Wow," Lauren said under her breath.

"This one's on me," Will said.

They walked up to the counter, and Lauren found herself praying there were rooms available—she could only imagine how nice the beds in this place were, and there was a Caribou Coffee in the lobby. She was already craving it tomorrow.

"And will you be attending our Christmas ball?" The man

behind the counter asked after Will told them they needed two rooms.

"No way. There's a Christmas ball?" He had that excited little kid thing going on again.

"Yes, sir. It's our premiere event of the season." He gave them a once-over, like the maître d' looking at Ferris Bueller while he claimed to be Abe Froman, the Sausage King of Chicago. "It's. . . ahem. . . a *dressy* affair."

They were certainly not dressy. Lauren was wearing her worn-out yoga pants and an old, pink Berkeley sweatshirt, and Will had on track pants and a black Nike hoodie.

"Yes, we will absolutely be attending." Will slapped the counter. "What time does it start?"

"Will—" Lauren smiled at the employee and pulled Will aside. "We can't go to a dance."

"It's like fate! What could bring more Christmas spirit than a Christmas ball in a fancy hotel?"

"I can think of about a thousand other things," she said.

"Name one."

Lauren paused. "Give me a second. . ."

"We're totally going."

Will stepped back up to the counter. "It's a yes on the ball, my friend."

The clerk slid their keys across the counter. "I gave you adjoining rooms."

"Oh, that isn't necessary," Lauren said.

"It's either that or you'll be on two different floors."

She smiled through a groan. "Perfect."

Those doors had locks on them, right?

They got in the elevator and took it to the twelfth floor. When they got out, Will handed her a small rectangular ticket. On it, the words "Twentieth Annual Brush Creek Christmas Ball."

"Will, I can't go to this!"

"Why not?"

"It's a *ball*."

"You say it like the Queen of England is throwing it."

"She may as well be!"

"I'll brush up on my British accent." He waggled his eyebrows. "Ooh, maybe you'll overhear Mr. Darcy say something horrible about you."

A faint memory crept in, but she shoved it aside and gave him a light push. "I have nothing to wear."

"Well, you'll have to wear *some*thing, I don't think it's that kind of ball."

"Will, I'm serious!"

"You don't have anything in that big, fat suitcase?" He eyed it suspiciously.

"For a dance? Are you kidding?" She shoved her key card in the door, waited for the green light to flicker and pushed it open.

"No little black dress?"

Dang it.

She put a hand on her hip and pressed her lips together, knowing full well she did, in fact, have a little black dress in her suitcase.

She'd packed it *just in case* because she was a person who liked to be prepared.

"Ha *ha*. I figured you'd have something. Since you're a person who likes to be prepared." He grinned.

It was eerie that he'd vocalized her exact thought.

"Take your time getting ready, and then knock on the door when you want to head down." He pointed to the door that connected their rooms.

"So, never, then?"

"Lauren." He backed slowly toward the door.

Her eyebrows shot up.

"Live a little, will ya?"

The door slowly shut on Will's double thumbs up and his stupid (adorable) grin.

Once alone, she turned, took two steps, and then flopped face first onto the giant king-sized bed. She spread her arms out wide and shouted "WHAT ARE YOU DOING?!" into the downy comforter. She flipped over, and wriggled a bit in the unfamiliar-but-insanely-comfortable bed. It practically begged her to take a nap and block out the rest of the world till morning.

But the man in the next room wasn't going to let that happen.

And she desperately didn't want to be boring.

She took the longest, hottest shower of her life, savoring every steamy minute. Their previous accommodations had been rudimentary at best, a lot like showering at what she imagined most outdoorsy dads would call a "nice campground." But this? This was borderline decadent.

After her shower, she slipped into the hotel robe and towel-dried her hair. She opened the bathroom door and watched the steam escape into the pristine hotel room.

Her phone dinged.

Text from Lisa to Lauren—6:43 PM

Lauren. . .!
Great news! The team at the network is looking for a head designer for a new show they're working on.
It's a sitcom about a mom who goes back to college at the same school as her daughter.
I recommended you for the job, showed them some of your work AND THEY WANT IT.
What do you think?

It was only after she read the text two more times that she realized she'd been holding her breath since she saw Lisa's name on her screen.

!!!

<huge smile emoji> I think you're ready.

Lisa!
YES.
And thank you!

Make sure you use some of your own artwork in this design too, okay?
It's perfect in the dorm, and it'll be perfect for this too.
<thumbs-up emoji>

How did you know?

I know everything *<winking emoji>*
Congrats!

CHAPTER 23

❄

Lauren turned a circle, and suddenly the room felt too big, too spacious. This was huge news! She called Maddie—straight to voicemail. Spencer—also voicemail. She clicked out of the call and went into her contacts, scrolling through names of co-workers, the pizza delivery place that was one of her "favorites", her next-door neighbor, Gladys Ripkin, all the while ignoring the nagging voice in the back of her head that practically shouted at her: *Go. Tell. Will!*

She was beaming, laughing out loud, and looking around for somewhere to scream the news. This was what she'd been working for—striving for—since she moved to LA. It was the thing that always seemed just out of her reach. And she'd done it.

I actually did it. All by myself!

This realization should've made her feel like Wonder Woman, but it didn't. Instead, she was sitting in a kitchen chair, listening to a slamming door, and watching her friends leave her birthday party one by one.

All. By. My. Self.

She was about to burst with this news, and she didn't want to *want* to tell Will.

But she did. She wanted to pound on his door and bubble over with excitement.

He would be genuinely thrilled with her about it. He'd proven that more than once since they left California. For all his faults, he seemed to be really good at this people thing. Lauren envied him that. It certainly wasn't her strength.

And sharing this news would, of course, require her to be vulnerable again—this time without the cover of darkness. Was she ready to do that?

With the exception of Maddie, most of Lauren's relationships stayed pretty close to the surface. And oh, the irony, the only other person who knew anything personal about her at all was in the next room.

That terrified her.

She'd done a terrible job of keeping him at an arm's length. Her feelings were back—she couldn't deny it. Before it was charm, and flirtation, and a very handsome face.

This time? It was so much more.

She scanned the upscale space, her gaze landing on the adjoining door that led to Will's room.

She stood in front of the door, hand poised to knock, when her phone dinged again. She picked it up and found a text from Will.

Hey, I'm dressed and ready.
No rush, but I'm going to head downstairs and look around a little.
If your dress isn't little and black go back and change! <winking with tongue out emoji>
Meet me in the restaurant when you can, Scrooge!

Lauren closed her eyes and breathed a trembling smile. She

felt like a kid in a tree, venturing out onto a branch, hoping it would hold her up.

Did she have the courage necessary to take a single step toward a genuine feeling?

To Lauren, this step on this limb meant everything.

She didn't know if she was ready, mentally or otherwise, to take this risk, but she wasn't going to let her fear stop her anymore. She thought herself flirty and tapped her reply.

> You're stuck with what I have on!
> <dancing lady emoji>
> Be down in a few!

With renewed courage, Lauren pulled her little black dress off the hanger. She'd only worn it a couple of times, but it fit her like a glove. Even she had to admit, it hugged her body in all the right places. This dress made her feel invincible, amorous, coy.

She dried and curled her hair, applied her makeup carefully—dabbing extra shadow on the lids, and using a darker line of eyeliner than her normal, barely-there application. She even fished a lipstick from her bag that hadn't seen the light of day in months. She found the one pair of heels she'd packed stashed at the bottom of her suitcase and gave herself a lingering, turning this-way-and-that, once-over in the full body mirror.

Compared to her daily attire, this was a major step-up. She felt pretty, an *anxious-to-see-Will's-reaction* pretty.

A connection to a covered memory pushed to the surface.

Who looks like a librarian now?

A familiar voice at the back of her mind whispered a warning. She was walking a very fine line. She might not say it out loud, but she clearly wanted to impress the only person she knew in this hotel.

Danger.

She smoothed her hands over her hips, running them

down her legs as she spun to face the back. *He's different now,* she thought. He cared about people—really cared about them.

And she'd opened up to him because he felt safe.

She grabbed her phone and snapped a picture of herself in the mirror, sent it to Maddie with an accompanying text:

> God help me, I'm going to go for it!

She pep-talked herself all the way to the elevator. She wasn't sure how to make her interest in him known, although she had a feeling her dress would handle the introduction. There had been moments, more than a few, where she thought maybe —*maybe*—he was thinking about kissing her. It was a foolish thought, but then he'd tucked her hair behind her ear and her entire body responded with a thundering Hallelujah chorus, and, of course, she'd gotten weird and awkward and changed the subject.

He wanted to kiss me and I talked about corn.

She leaned against the back of the elevator and groaned.

Nope. Done. Done with all of that mess. Done being awkward. Done being the wallflower. It was time to bloom.

If only she had any idea what that meant.

She tried out a few scenarios in her head. She wouldn't throw herself at him, no way she'd be just like all the other girls. He should make the first move. But she had to make him *want* to make the first move.

Maybe he'd take one look at her and that would be enough.

Or maybe he'd ask her to dance—which could *lead* to a kiss, which she wouldn't stop.

She smiled at her reflection in the golden mirror of the elevator wall. An acapella version of "I'll Be Home for Christmas" played on the speaker overhead, and she caught herself humming along with it.

The next time Will made her sing for her coffee, this would be the song she chose.

The elevator dinged, and she stepped out. She walked toward the restaurant, feeling like she was floating on air. She made her way through the lobby, admiring the Christmas decorations and the care it must've taken to make this place look so beautiful. She knew a person had to have the perfect balance of creativity and attention to detail to pull off décor as intricate as this.

She wasn't sure, but things seemed brighter. Colors popped more than they had when they'd checked in. The lights weren't just on, they sparkled.

Her thoughts were interrupted as she reached the doorway of the restaurant and stood by the host stand, looking around the modern space. She scanned the tables—mostly occupied, buzzing conversation, clinking silverware—but didn't see Will. Maybe this moment would be like that moment in *Pretty Woman* where Richard Gere saw Julia Roberts in that red dress and couldn't believe the girl he'd picked up on the street had it in her to look like *this*.

Wait. Perhaps a different analogy. Comparing herself to a hooker probably wasn't the most romantic notion.

She saw Will—and the whole notion of romance was knocked right out of her mind.

She spotted him, back to her, sitting at the bar, laughing with a tall blonde wearing a skimpy, low-cut red dress and heels that had to be impossible to walk in.

Lauren was no body language expert, but the way the blonde leaned toward him reminded her a lot of a lioness stalking her prey.

Maybe it's fine, maybe I'm just misinterpr—

Will said something, and the woman threw her head back in laughter, then let her hand rest on his arm, a lingering touch that even Lauren knew spoke volumes.

The branch she'd tenderly tested her weight on broke underneath her.

She was falling. Again. Falling for him and falling apart. All at once, she was eighteen, a stupid girl with a stupid crush who believed that someone like Will might actually see her as anything more than his best friend's kid sister.

She'd given him way too much credit.

People don't change.

Flirts flirt. Players play. Charmers charm.

And girls like Lauren? They get their heart broken because they always seem to try and give it to the wrong people.

"Miss, are you looking for someone?" The host had returned to his station.

She felt like an idiot. She'd gotten dressed up—put on lipstick, for Pete's sake—and for what? For *what??*

What was I thinking?

She was thinking she was tired of being alone, of being closed off, of spending all her time on work and never on herself. She was thinking how nice it would be if she had someone to celebrate with. Not just anyone—Will. Because he still made her palms sweat and her pulse race.

"Miss?" the host repeated.

"No." She backed away, holding up a shaky hand and holding back her tears. "Sorry. I'm not looking for anyone."

She walked out into the lobby and texted Will.

> Sorry, I think I got a migraine.
> I'll have to take a rain check on the ball.

NOOOO
Lauren!
I'm coming up to get you.

> Absolutely do not do that.

> I'm serious, I don't feel well.

Can I get you anything?
I can order some soup or something? Does soup help a migraine?

Lauren felt the hot coals of his kindness heaped on her head.

> No, thanks.
> I just need to sleep it off.
> I'll see you in the morning.
> Maybe we can make it home tomorrow?

<eyes wide emoji>
But. . .I got all dressed up.

She didn't text him back. She didn't know what to say. After a few minutes, her phone vibrated for the second to last time that night.

We can try to make it home tomorrow.
Sleep well, Lo.
I hope you feel better.
<heart emoji>

CHAPTER 24

❄

Will tucked the phone back in his pocket, disappointed. He'd been looking forward to spending the evening with Lauren. Even though she was sometimes standoffish, he liked her company.

He also was a little excited about going to a Christmas ball—though not his first choice of entertainment.

It would've felt a lot like a date.

And yeah, he wanted to find out what that would be like.

The woman who had slithered up beside him—*'Call me Gin, like the drink'*—made a pouty face. "Everything okay? You look disappointed."

He knew her type. In a past life, he might've found flirting with her worth his time, but in the moment, the only thing he wanted to do was go back to the twelfth floor and see if he could do anything to help Lauren.

"I'm fine," he said.

"Was that your friend?" she asked, nodding toward his phone.

He nodded. "Yeah, she's not feeling well."

"*Girl*friend?"

Will glanced her way without saying anything and put the phone back in his pocket.

"Awww." Gin feigned disappointment. "Well, she obviously doesn't know what she has." Her hand was back on his arm. "Guess it's just you and me, then. I've never been to a Christmas ball."

His laugh sounded nervous—he was so out of practice. And this conversation felt off, like he'd accidentally put his shoes on the wrong feet. "Actually," he got the bartender's attention with a wave, "I think I'm going to call it a night."

She frowned. "So early? You look like you could use a little fun."

He turned and faced her. "I'm really tired." He reached into his jacket pocket, pulled out the tickets to the dance, and then nodded to the end of the bar where a lonely-looking guy sat, nursing a drink. "Ask that guy. He looks like he could use some company."

Gin tossed a dismissive glance toward Lonely Man, then looked Will up and down. "Mmm, that's not a fair trade."

Will was beginning to get annoyed. He found himself not caring in the slightest if this woman liked him or not.

Strange.

He slipped his arm from her grasp and didn't smile. "That's as good as it's gonna get, I'm afraid."

The pouty lip was out again. He couldn't imagine Lauren ever fake-pouting to try and manipulate someone. But then, Lauren was a grown-up. She'd been a grown-up since she was eleven years old.

Maybe that's why he liked her. She didn't try to be someone she wasn't. These little games other women played were completely foreign to her.

It was one of the things he admired most.

He set the tickets on the bar and loosened his tie as he walked toward the elevator. At the ding of the twelfth floor, he got out and stopped in front of Lauren's door. He stood there for at least two straight minutes, wondering if he should knock. She probably wanted to be alone—he knew migraines could be brutal, but he couldn't deny that he wanted her to let him in so he could take care of her.

It had been less than a week, but he hadn't felt this way before. Lauren had always been a sort of mystery to him, even when they were younger, but he'd never acted on that curiosity out of respect for Spencer—but now that he was an adult, now that he'd figured out who he was and what he wanted (*and didn't want, "Gin like the drink"*) out of a relationship, he couldn't stop thinking about her.

Before he lost his nerve, he knocked on the door lightly, waiting for any sign of life on the other side. When none came, he opened his own door and slipped inside, then listened at the door adjoining their two rooms. Only silence.

He flipped on the television, undressed, and tried to sleep. When he couldn't, he pulled out his phone, and held it, wondering what he could text that would make her feel any better. He didn't feel witty, so he just texted a heart.

After another half-hour of waiting for a reply, Will finally put his phone up and forced his eyes closed.

∼

The next morning, Will found Lauren packed and ready to go, sitting in the coffee shop, working on her computer—very large cup of coffee at her side.

He rolled his own suitcase toward her and sat down. She didn't look up.

"How are you feeling?" he asked.

"Great." Still no eye contact. "Did you have fun at the ball?"

He situated his suitcase between his chair and the window. "Oh, I gave the tickets away."

Her eyes darted to his, then back to her screen.

"No point going alone."

Her scoff was so soft he almost missed it. "I'm sure you could've found company."

"Not company worth having," he said.

Her shoulders lowered ever so slightly, but still, she avoided his eyes.

"What are you working on?" He watched as she continued pecking away on the keyboard.

"I was just hired as the head set decorator on a new show." Her tone was clipped, matter-of-fact. "So, I'm getting a head start on brainstorming. I don't want to fall any farther behind than I already am taking so much time off."

"Wait." He reached over and closed her laptop. "*Head* set decorator? I thought you were an assistant."

She pressed her lips together and leveled his gaze. "I was. And now I'm not."

"Lauren, that's amazing." He frowned. "This is a good thing, right?"

"It's a great thing." She started packing her computer in its case. "It's just a lot more responsibility, and I want to get it right." Beside her computer, he saw now, was her sketch pad—and on it, a rendering of a room that looked professionally drawn.

He was beginning to see why she was confident in her work —she was really, really good at what she did.

He reached across the table and put a hand on hers. She froze. "You're going to be amazing at this, you know that right? We need to celebrate."

"No. It's fine. Let's just get going." She stood.

"Lo, you gotta take time to celebrate this. These kinds of wins only come along so many times in your life."

"Maybe I'll celebrate when the job is finished and everyone

is happy with what I've done." She slung her bag over her shoulder. "But right now, I just want to get home."

And with that, she walked away. Whatever bridge had been built between them seemed to have been blown up overnight, and Will had no idea why.

He ordered his coffee to go and found her waiting outside near the sidewalk. Even in her fleece pajama pants and ratty old sweatshirt she looked sort of incredible. It was something about the way the morning light hit her. Or the messy ponytail. Or the sunglasses that hid half of her face.

Or maybe, it was simply something about Lauren.

He'd fallen for her, and he had no idea how to proceed. With caution, he assumed. He felt like a sacrificial rat sniffing out live mines in a field.

They walked to the repair shop where—thankfully—the Grand Cherokee was waiting for them. He paid for the new tire and found Lauren in the parking lot.

"You okay?" He unlocked the car.

"Yeah," she said absently. "Just have a lot on my mind." She stuffed her bags into the back, then opened the passenger side door. He put a hand on her arm, and again, her muscles tensed.

"I'm really excited for you, Lauren. You've been working hard for this, and it's a huge deal. Don't pretend like it's not."

She held his gaze, and he could see thoughts tumbling around in her mind, but in response, she simply put on a clearly fake smile and said, "Thanks." Then got in the car.

Square one.

They were back where they'd started. As if they'd never shared a single moment on common ground.

And he had no idea how to fix it.

CHAPTER 25

Lauren's reinstated resolve was wavering with every touch, every kind word Will said to her. She knew he didn't stay downstairs and hook up with that leggy blonde because she heard his knock on her door about twenty minutes after she texted. She knew he couldn't sleep because she'd laid there, awake, listening to the sound of his television through the wall.

She couldn't be sure, but she thought he was watching *Die Hard*. The first one.

And she saw his last text—a heart emoji—come in when her phone lit up on the nightstand.

She also knew she had no right to be mad at him. And yet, she couldn't be nice to him. She had no idea what had stopped her from answering his knock last night. Only that she'd let herself think about him—dream about him—in a way she swore she would never do again.

This is stupid. What am I doing? Why am I like this?

Will had a magnetic charm that women were drawn to. There would always be a leggy blonde or a stunning brunette or a flirty redhead to compete with. And she knew she'd never come out ahead.

Still, the silence made her even sadder. She missed their banter. She even missed Will singing off-key.

She missed Will, and he was sitting right next to her.

She didn't know how to be friends with him without falling for him.

Will didn't stop nearly as many times as he had on their previous travel days; Lauren guessed it was because of her bad attitude. But around noon, he pulled off for gas and food at a little café next to a fudge factory.

The air between them was superficially cordial. He was acting like he was invited to a wedding and didn't know anyone at his table. The walk to the door was tense and she hated that it was her fault.

She pretended to engross herself in her phone, hyper-aware that he was watching her. Their food came, and she preceded to push it around her plate without really eating.

And still he watched her. Finally, she met his gaze.

"You're staring at me."

He nodded. "I am."

She looked around, avoiding his eyes. "Why?"

He narrowed his eyes. "I'm trying to figure out what's wrong with you."

"Nothing's wrong," she brushed off. "I told you, I'm just stressed out."

"No. This is different. You're being all closed off and rude again, like you were at the beginning of this trip."

She shrugged. "What makes you think anything's changed since then?"

Lauren, good grief, that was mean.

"Oh, I don't know, maybe because everything *did* change." He looked genuinely hurt by her cold shoulder.

Something inside her twisted at the thought.

She wasn't this person. She wasn't mean. She didn't

purposely wound people who'd done nothing but be nice to her. "Will, let's not pretend—"

"Yes, Lauren, let's not." His tone mocked her.

She stalled, unsure what to say.

"Let's not pretend that there isn't something going on here." He flicked a hand back and forth between them, as if they were a pair.

She frowned. "What?"

"You and me," he said. "We like each other, right? Or did I have that completely wrong?"

Her pulse quickened, but her brain slowed. She scrambled for an answer, and found nothing.

"You're one of the most mature people I know, but right now you're acting like a child."

She could hardly believe it. "I'm the child. *I'm* the child? What about you?"

"What about me?" He seemed genuinely confused.

"You have nothing to say?"

"What are you talking about?"

"I saw you, Will!" She regretted the words as soon as they were out.

He looked around, as if trying to find the answer laying on the floor in the room. "Saw me where?"

"Nowhere. Just forget it."

This was so dumb. She scolded herself in her head. Her fear and her pride were going to kill this relationship before it even started.

She had no right to feel the way she did, and yet, this was how she felt. Seeing him at the bar was like seeing him in the kitchen.

The girl even had the same color hair.

How do you tell someone they broke your heart when they don't even remember the night it happened? How do you explain this was the *only way* to keep it from happening again?

How do you admit feelings you really, really didn't want to have?

"Lauren. Something is obviously bothering you. I can't help if you won't talk."

A traitorous knot tied itself at the base of her throat. He was right, she was acting like a child. This was the part of the movie where everyone watching screams "Just tell him already!"

Heck, even she was internally screaming that. But stopping that meant talking, and talking meant opening up, and opening up meant hurt.

"It's nothing. I'm just dealing with some stuff."

"What stuff?"

"Personal stuff. I'll stop taking it out on you."

"Lauren, I don't care if you take it out on me, but I can't fight a battle that I don't even know I'm in."

He watched her, and she nearly shrunk under his gaze.

"Lauren, I like you."

Her eyes shot to his, as if somehow, she had the ability to deduce whether he was being sincere. She wasn't a good judge and she knew it.

"What do you mean?"

And that's when he smiled, and her stomach flip-flopped, and the cage she'd built around her heart began to crack.

"I mean, I like you. Is that so hard to believe?"

"Actually, yes."

"Don't get me wrong, you're a huge pain, a horrible traveler, and you drive me absolutely crazy." He reached across the table and took her hand. "But I can't stop thinking about you. You are who you say you are. You don't try to be something you're not or waste time playing games. You're smart, and you don't pretend you're not. You're beautiful, but you have no idea. You know what you want, and you go for it."

"That's not true," she said quietly.

"Seems like it to me."

"But you don't know what I want." She looked up, desperate, and found his eyes.

He took a calming breath. "Then tell me."

She wanted to, so badly. The words were right there, *right there*, about to spill out of her like a tipped-over bucket of water.

"Can we go outside?"

He nodded immediately. "Sure."

They paid their check, then walked in silence to the Jeep. He was waiting for her to say something, and she wasn't sure she could. Her emotions were on the spin cycle.

She looked around, trying to find a hiding place.

"I saw you last night with that woman," she finally blurted.

No going back now.

He looked at her, and she looked away, hating how naked she felt at the admission she'd been bothered at all. Admitting how it made her feel meant admitting she had feelings to betray. It was a whole lot of transparency, and she wasn't ready for it.

"Wait. Gin?"

"What?"

"That woman. Her name was Gin."

"Her name was *what*?" Lauren scoffed as she said it.

"I don't know her," Will said. "She sat down next to me and started talking to me, and wait—is this why you bailed on the Christmas dance?"

She looked away.

"Lauren," he took a step toward her. "I was waiting for you. I told her that the second she sat down."

"She must not have heard you," Lauren said. "I saw you and you said something and she laughed and she had her hand on your arm and—ugh—it doesn't even matter! I have no right to be upset. If you want to go out with some stranger in a hotel, that's your prerogative."

"I didn't want to go out with some stranger in a hotel. I wanted to go out with you!" He took her by the shoulders and forced her gaze. "I've always had a thing for you. Always wondered what it would be like if something happened between us."

She flinched, as if physically hit, and pulled away.

"What's wrong?"

She glared. "That's exactly what you said to me that night."

"What night?" His eyes searched hers.

"Word for word, Will. *Word for word!*" She turned a circle, feeling trapped in a city that wasn't her own.

"Lauren, what night?" He looked desperate for answers only she had.

She looked away, then directly in his eyes. "The night you kissed me."

Will's brows pulled downward in a tight V. "What are you talking about?" He paused, a look of horror on his face, then turned serious. "Lauren, you have to explain this to me. What are you talking about?"

She shoved her hands through her hair. "You were drunk!" She crossed her arms over her chest. "The party? I saw you at a party, and you asked me to drive you home. . ." Her vulnerability made her shake.

He took a step away from her. He put his head down, and softly said, "But there's more."

She'd never considered this might be as hard for him to hear as it was for her to say.

She closed her eyes.

So, they were doing this. She was going to tell him everything—finally—words she swore she'd never say out loud. Words she couldn't keep inside any longer.

CHAPTER 26

❄

In a flash, she was on holiday break from college her freshman year. Lauren hadn't stayed close to home—why would she? She wanted to study film. And she'd taken to Berkeley almost instantly. A lot of her friends had trouble adjusting, off at school in a different state, but she took to being away like Andy Dufresne spreading his arms wide in the rain after crawling through the sewer pipe at the end of *The Shawshank Redemption*.

Free.

She'd only gone home because everyone else was going home. The dorms were closing, and what was she going to do on campus alone for an entire month?

It was her second night back when she was invited to a holiday party at Annabelle DeVore's house. She wanted her classmates to see how well she was doing, that she'd blossomed (*finally*) and become more than just the bookish valedictorian they all thought they knew.

She walked in and spotted her friend Mai Li, who had also thrived being away, but who apparently was a lot more into partying than she had been when they were in high school.

Lauren was used to being the only sober person by the end of a night out with her friends, and she took her designated driver job very seriously. She supposed it shouldn't be any different now—she really didn't have any desire to make a complete fool of herself.

But when she walked in and saw Will standing next to the keg, she almost—*almost*—changed her mind.

He appeared to be a lot farther along in his alcohol consumption than just about everyone else in the room, and when he spotted her, he lifted both arms, spilling his drink. "Richmond!"

She waved back, and heard him say, "It's Spencer's little sister!"

The night wore on, and Lauren grew increasingly aware of Will, paying far more attention than she should've to where he was at all times.

He wasn't just drunk—he was plastered. Wasted. In full-on self-destruct mode. If Spencer had been there, he would've known what to do, but he wasn't due home until the following day. She was on her own.

And on her own with Will Sinclair was not a good place for her to be.

Around midnight, Will plopped down on the couch next to Lauren and wrapped an arm around her. "Can you give me a ride? I haff t' go home now. I can't stay here because this issin't my house."

She had seen this behavior before with her friends many, many times. She pulled back, speaking slowly. "Sure, Will. I've got my car."

"This issin't my house." He paused, trying to focus on her face. "Can you take me home?" He paused, confused. "Did I just ask you that?"

At least he knew better than to drive.

"Yes. You did. I can take you, no problem."

He pointed a wavy finger at her. "Ahhhh. . .*Spencer's little sister!*"

She stood, pulled her purse up over her shoulder, and helped him to his feet. She made sure Mai Li had a safe way home, and finally, with some effort, and lots of stopping for him to high-five other guys at the party, they made it to her car.

Inside, Lauren felt the acute weight of his presence. She told herself this was nothing—she was practically the only sober person at that party—of course he would ask her for a ride home.

Lauren drove. She was looking straight ahead, but Will was looking at *her*. And his attention made her feel slightly intoxicated herself. She was that eleven-almost-twelve-year-old girl all over again, seeing him for the first time and imagining the day he finally—*finally* saw her as more than just his best friend's dorky little sister.

Was that day finally here?

"You're pretty, you know that?" He reached over and touched a strand of her hair.

"And you're drunk." She gently put his hand back on his side of the car. She really hoped he, and her heart, were both getting the message.

"I'm not. . .so out of it I can't see someone who's beautiful and right'n front of me," he spoke with the effort of someone desperately trying to walk a straight line. He leaned back in the seat with a sigh. "I know what I see. Dussn't mean I don't know what I'm sayin'."

She'd never been drunk, and she wondered if alcohol made you lie or if it made you more honest.

Lauren drove on, in tense silence, finally turning on his street. She parked her car in front of his house and avoided his eyes. "You're home now."

Silence stretched.

She finally risked a glance, but his eyes were closed. Was he snoring? She poked his shoulder. "Will?"

He stirred—barely—and she panicked. How was she going to get him out of her car?

"Will, you need to go in now."

No response.

She groaned, opened the car door, and hurried around to the passenger side. She pulled his door open and he nearly fell out onto the pavement. She righted him, ignoring the fact that this was the closest she'd ever been to him in her life.

"Wow, you smell good." He stuck his face in her hair and inhaled.

"We need to get you inside."

"*Okay, Spencer's little sister. . .!*" He said it like a secret.

She shushed him, as she helped him out of the car and to his feet. "You're going to wake everyone up."

He stuck a finger in front of his mouth and made a "shushing" noise, then chuckled to himself.

She looped an arm around his waist, and he draped an arm around her shoulders. He was significantly bigger than she was, but she managed to help him up the porch stairs. At the front door, she stopped. "Can you take it from here?"

He tipped forward and leaned his head against the siding.

So, that's a no.

She peeked in the windows, but the lights were off. Everyone appeared to be in bed for the night.

"Okay, I'll help you. Just be quiet, okay?"

He shushed again in response.

She pulled the door open and helped him through, closing it as quietly as she could behind them. "Where's your room?" she whispered.

He pointed to the stairs, and she shouldered as much of his weight as she could as she led him over and up. They were doing fine until he stumbled and knocked a framed photo of a young Will in a baseball jersey smiling at the camera off the wall. It clattered to the floor, and they both froze, but remarkably, nobody appeared in the hallway. No lights flipped on.

"Sorry," he hissed.

"Just keep moving." She pulled him up the stairs and down the hallway, past a closed door, where she assumed someone was sleeping. At the end of the hall, she followed his point through an open door, deposited him on the bed, then plopped down next to him, slightly out of breath. She flipped on the lamp beside his bed and looked around the room.

The walls were plastered with baseball posters, framed cards—some signed—and there were three autographed baseballs displayed in glass boxes on his dresser. She knew Will loved baseball—it was like he was born to play. She'd gone to lots of his games, towed by Spencer, secretly loving every minute. How many times had she watched him in rousing victory, then watched him head off with the rest of the team to a party she wasn't invited to and wouldn't dare show up at?

And now, here she was, the only one with his attention. It made her feel special.

A misguided feeling, but she didn't care. Not in the moment.

He rolled over closer to her and sat up. She realized, in her periphery, he was looking at her, fully awake despite his intoxication.

"You're pretty great, Lauren Richmond." He gently reached up, hesitated a beat, then brushed her hair back away from her face, grazing her skin as he did. Her breath shuddered at his touch.

She dared a glance in his direction and found him studying her. Her mouth went dry.

"Why didn't I see you before?" It seemed he was honestly asking. He was suddenly clear. No slurring, no wavering.

She laughed, nervously. "I'm easy to miss."

He shook his head. "No. You're not. You're just way too good for most guys."

"That's not true," she said.

"Do you have a boyfriend?" he asked abruptly.

She felt her head shake a 'no.'

He smiled a half smile. "So, nobody will get mad if I kiss you?"

She thought of Spencer. He would get mad, but he didn't get a say, no matter how much he thought he did. She shook her head again, and Will took her face in his hands and kissed her so softly it made the hair on the back of her neck stand up. He moved from her lips to her neck to the soft spot just below her ear, then pulled back to look at her again. "You really are beautiful, Lauren."

She'd never been one of those dopey girls, the kind who squealed and swooned, but in that moment, that's exactly what she became.

Will slowly pulled her body into his. She didn't put up a fight.

She fell, headfirst, into the moment. She'd dreamed of this for as long as she could remember, using her fantasies about Will as a way to escape the bad parts of her life. Without knowing it, he'd comforted her. Gave her something good to get lost in for a while.

And now, he'd seen her—he'd seen her, and finally, he'd realized they were perfect for each other.

He reached over and turned off the lamp, then leaned back, drawing her toward him. All her defenses unraveled right there in that room. His lips, soft and full, searched hers, as if he'd found something worth exploring. As if he had an insatiable desire—for her.

Lying there beside him, his arms wrapped around her, relishing the way his lips felt on hers, Lauren left her own body for a minute and let herself believe that this could happen—they could actually make this work. Everything she'd been hoping for was finally, finally coming true.

They kissed so fully, so intensely and for so long, they pushed each other away to catch their collective breath. Seconds later, she kissed him again. She liked kissing him—loved kissing him. She didn't ever want it to end. She smiled against his lips and said, "You don't know how many times I've dreamed of this. Me and you, together. We would be so good together, wouldn't we?"

He kissed her again, this time soft and sweet, running his hand down her cheek, her neck, his eyes so bright they practically lit up the dark room.

"I've always had a thing for you," he said. "Always wondered what it would be like if something happened between us."

"Really?" She touched his cheek, lost in him. "Me too."

"Good." Another kiss.

"But I can't sleep with you," she said. "That's okay, right?"

His brow furrowed. "Yeah, of course."

She kissed him again. "Good, because you're drunk and I've never—" She chose not to finish the sentence.

They laid there in the dark for a long moment, their breathing, the only sound that cut through the silence.

"I would just want it to mean something," she said.

"Me too, Lo," he said.

They lay like that for several minutes, the black of the room making it impossible to see anything other than outlines.

"I should probably go," she finally said, wishing she could stay.

He looked her square in the face and smiled. "Thanks for getting me home safe and sound."

She leaned in and kissed him again, her heart swirling with happiness. "You'll call me tomorrow?"

"I promise." His face was so earnest, he had to mean it.

He had to, right?

"You don't have to walk me out," she said, dreamily. "I know the way."

Back in the safety of her car, Lauren held her breath. She replayed the moments over and over, feeling his lips again and again. She let out a tiny, happy squeal—just like all the girls she couldn't relate to. The ones whose identities were wrapped up in some guy. She'd joined their club. She understood now why they acted the way they did.

Did that really just happen? Did Will Sinclair just kiss me?

Not just kissed her, either—but *kissed* her. The kind of kiss that made her want to collapse into a heap on the floor. The kind of kiss she felt in her toes. The kind of kiss that ruined her for all future kisses.

Am I...with Will Sinclair now?

Will Sinclair had kissed her. He said he thought about her. He said he'd call her. After all the horrible Christmases, all of the present-less mornings, the yelling and fighting, the pretending and hiding—maybe Christmas wasn't so bad after all.

She woke late the next morning.

Will.

The sun was streaming through her window—but she was still living in the dark warmth of his room.

"I've always had a thing for you," he had said. He said that. To me.

Lauren waited. She waited for him to call, to text, to stop by. She waited.

Will didn't call. Not that day. Not the next day.

Not the day after that, either.

After seven days—a full week since she'd driven him home—she overheard Spencer talking about a party he was going to with Will. She burned with hurt, and before she thought better, she got in her car and drove to the party.

She had to talk to Will.

Lauren walked into the crowded house, wall-to-wall people,

and she pressed her way through the crowd of sweaty alcohol and red Solo cups. A player she recognized from Spencer's baseball team turned suddenly and spilled his drink all over her shirt.

"Oh, man, I'm so sorry." Clumsy started patting her chest with a napkin, and she pushed him, violated, hot tears stinging her eyes.

"Back off!" she shouted over the noise.

"Sorry." He held up two hands in surrender, then righted the Santa hat on his head.

She stuck out her chin. "Have you seen Will Sinclair?"

"Nah," Clumsy said, as a guy they called "Tank" walked by, overhearing.

"You looking for Will?" Tank asked.

She nodded. "Yeah, have you seen him?"

Tank laughed. "Check with her." He pointed across the room at a thin blond cheerleader who'd graduated the year ahead of Lauren.

"Kaitlyn! This chick, sorry what's your name again—?"

"*Lauren.*"

"—yeah, Lauren, right, she's looking for Will," Tank shouted over the din.

Lauren's face heated as the girl looked her up and down, grimaced, then said, "Why?"

"Why are you looking for him? Are you like, his tutor or something?" Clumsy asked.

She'd never felt more out of place in her life.

Lauren's face heated with irritation. "I just need to talk to him." Lauren pushed her way past them, eyes scanning, but there was no Will. And thankfully, no Spencer either. Maybe they were together. Maybe they'd decided not to come to this stupid party at all. Maybe Will was telling Spencer how he really felt about her—making sure it was cool with her brother if the two of them were a couple.

She made her way around the whole house, decked out for Christmas, only a few days away now, but there was no sign, and then walked by the kitchen.

"Can you explain why that loser of a girl is looking for you?" The accusation stopped Lauren just outside the room. She stayed behind the doorjamb, hidden from sight but with a clear view into the kitchen. She listened over the noise of the party.

"I don't even know who you're talking about."

Will.

"Well, she apparently knows *you*. Some girl named *Lauren* or something?"

"Wait. Spencer's little sister?"

Lauren's face flushed.

"I guess," Kaitlyn cracked. "What is she doing here and why is she asking for you?"

Will scoffed. "I don't know why she's here—I didn't invite her."

Lauren's muscles tensed—she was so thankful for the wall between them right now.

"Well, she's *here* somewhere. For you. Care to explain?"

Will, you said that you always wondered about me. . . please just say that you want me and not her please. . .

A pause. "Kaitlyn, do you really think there's something going on with me and Lauren Richmond?" Another pause. "I've known her my whole life—she's like my little sister."

No.

Kaitlyn cocked a hip, toeing one foot and draping an arm on Will's neck. "You promise?"

"Are you worried?"

She leaned against the wall, heart racing. *Will, PLEASE!*

"I guess not. It's not like you'd date a girl like her, anyway. She looks like a *librarian*."

Kaitlyn turned away, teasing. "Some guys fantasize about librarians, you know."

"Only if they're hot." He tugged at Kaitlyn's waist, drawing her body to his.

Lauren wanted to die. No amount of willpower could stop her from crying.

"I can think of a million other things I'd rather be doing with you right now," Will said, "and none of them involves talking."

As Lauren leaned against the wall and closed her eyes, stormy tears slid down her cheeks.

"Hey, I found Will!" Clumsy was back, and now he stood in the doorway, threatening to reveal her hiding place, just out of sight. He looked at Lauren, then into the kitchen. "You still want him?"

She pushed herself up off the wall and wiped her cheeks. "No. I *definitely* don't want him."

She rushed out of the house and back into the quiet comfort of her car.

Her car that still, if she inhaled deeply enough, smelled like Will.

She dropped her forehead onto the steering wheel and cried —the kind of tears that burst, mottling her jeans in a haphazard pattern. She slammed her palm on the dashboard twice, hard.

I am such an idiot!

She wasn't special. He hadn't thought about her. He didn't even remember.

He wasn't the guy she'd built him up to be, and he certainly wasn't the guy she thought he was.

In that moment she decided to stop caring about Will Sinclair. She would start systematically replacing all the fantasies of him, beginning with that conversation in the kitchen. She started her car, put it in drive, and drove away, leaving the house and Will in her rearview mirror.

Until this trip.

CHAPTER 27

❄

The truth, like an undertow, seemed to have staggered Will.

The parking lot of the little diner had gone quiet, the chocolatey smell that wafted out of the fudge factory less enticing than when they'd arrived.

"Lauren, I—" His voice gave out. He pressed his palms into his eyes, then dragged his hands down his face. "Did we. . .?"

"No, nothing like that." Lauren shifted, feeling exposed.

He looked desperately at her, the flashing sign above the diner catching her eye.

"Will, *no*. We didn't."

Obvious relief washed over him. He hung his head.

The floodgates were open now. No truth would remain covered.

She cleared her throat. "Before, when I was younger, I *really* liked you. I was infatuated with you, but I think it had more to do with your looks. This time it wasn't just about a physical attraction for me."

She took a small step, trying to get him to look up.

"Will, I think I've loved you since the day I met you."

The admission hung between them, but saying it in this context altered the meaning. "I built you up in my mind to be something, I don't know, like, untouchable. A perfect version of what I wanted. And that night, you were."

He finally looked up at her, pained. This was hard for them both.

"After that night, though, I finally realized it was a stupid little crush on someone who, let's be honest, didn't even know I existed."

He laughed ironically, shaking his head. "Yeah, that's the funny thing. I *did* know you existed. I saw you, Lauren." He looked away. He leaned against the SUV, regret clear on his face.

She winced. They were saying all the right things at completely the wrong time.

"And now I screwed that up, too," he said ruefully. "How many things can I completely sabotage? Dreams? Check. Career? Check. Lov—" he glanced at Lauren but stopped before he finished the word. He clenched his jaw and turned away, seemingly disgusted with himself.

Everything was out, laid bare. She'd been holding this all in for so long, and now that it was out in the open, she had no idea what to say next. Where did they go from here?

She knew where she needed to go. Right next to Will.

She moved into the space beside him, leaning against his Jeep, their shoulders touching.

"I hate that I hurt you." He looked at her, pleading forgiveness with his watery eyes. "I *hate* it."

She took a breath and a chance. "It's okay."

It wasn't. And yet, a part of her did feel lighter for having unloaded this burden. She'd had no closure up until this point.

But now, she did.

Would that wipe the hurt away? Could she hope to have the

weight lifted, the shades pulled back, simply by speaking her pain aloud?

"I think if it hadn't happened, I would've carried a torch for you all these years. I wouldn't have moved on, gotten to where I am now. It helped me, in a messed-up way, you know?"

He didn't take it as a compliment. "Yeah, I sure helped you move on by acting like a complete jerk. You deserved better."

He turned to her. "No. You *deserve* better. Better than me, that's for sure."

She paused, then said, "For the record, I don't think that's who you are anymore."

He fidgeted with his key fob. Looked defeated. "Like you said—people don't change." He pushed himself up off the vehicle and faced her. "For what it's worth—and this is long overdue—I'm really, really sorry that I hurt you."

"Thanks for saying that."

He looked down. "So. . .what now? What are we? Friends?"

She smiled a small smile. "I think that's a great place to start."

He held out his hand, dispassionately. "Well, then, hi. I'm Will Sinclair. Nice to meet you."

She slipped her hand in his hand. It was warm, but she noticed a slight tremor.

Is he. . .nervous?

"Lauren Richmond. It's nice to be met."

She held his hand for longer than a moment. Then, he let go, nodded, and said, "We should go."

"Yeah. We should." He walked to the other side of the SUV, and a thought struck her.

"Hey, Will."

He stopped. "Yeah?"

She smirked. "Can I drive?"

He laughed, and it looked like he needed it.

Wow, the roles have reversed.

"Absolutely not."

She hopped in the Jeep, a feeling in her stomach. It was a strange feeling—both lighter for having unloaded her emotions and heavier with the weight of his.

CHAPTER 28

❄

Will reeled at this new information.

How was it possible he'd been so cruel? How was it possible he didn't even remember? Knowing he'd hurt her—a completely innocent, witty, smart, beautiful girl—it nearly left him undone.

He had made bad choices. Period, full stop. But up until this point, he'd believed his choices only hurt himself. Being confronted with the truth that he'd hurt other people was the most difficult thing of all. The damage he'd done made him sick.

And he had no idea how to make it up to her.

So, they drove in silence.

He only stopped for gas and restrooms.

Will drove, tormented by the harsh reality that the choices of his twenty-one-year-old self were affecting his thirty-two-year-old life today. The thing that killed him the most was that he liked Lauren. A lot. It wasn't fair that his past should dictate his current situation, but it did. There was no way he could ask her to give him a chance now.

His penance was sacrificing his new feelings for her.

She said she's loved me since the first time she saw me. And Will knew exactly the day she was talking about.

She handed him a Coke in the kitchen.

How could he not have known? If he had treated her the way she deserved, his whole life would be different.

But he didn't. And he didn't deserve her. Not then and not now.

No wonder Spencer had made him promise.

He stopped for a handful more photos on the way, mostly because he had to finish what he'd started—but the joy of this trip had been left behind in the parking lot of a little café in Missouri.

They entered Illinois, and he pointed to the green and white sign, with "The Land of Lincoln" on it. "Hey, look, almost home."

She sighed a heavy sigh. "Yeah."

Driving from the bottom to the top of Illinois was a long prospect even on the best of days, but Will felt this last leg of their trip interminable.

Finally, after almost a week in the car (*and what felt like another week in just Illinois*) They pulled off the interstate toward Pleasant Valley. It was well after dark, and as he parked in front of his house, it gently started to snow. Big, fat, Illinois flakes that stuck in crystal clumps.

Snow had a way of covering things up and quieting the world. Will said a silent prayer that it would carry with it some magic that cleaned slates, too.

Lauren got out of the car and tipped her head back, giant flakes landing in her hair and on her eyelashes. The lamppost overhead bathed her in white light, and she smiled.

In that moment, Lauren Richmond looked more beautiful than anything Will Sinclair had ever seen. It was a cruel reminder that what he wanted was right in front of him—and still just out of his reach.

She stood like that for several seconds, unbothered, it seemed, by the cold.

"I forgot how much I missed snow." She spun in a slow circle, and he resisted the overwhelming urge to take her in his arms and tell her everything he was thinking. His spiraling thoughts needed a place to land.

He mentally kicked himself again.

She deserves so much better.

The door to his parents' house opened, and his mom shouted from the porch. "You're home!" Then, over her shoulder, "Will's home!"

Lauren's eyes popped open, and the smile faded from her face. She looked around, then said quietly, "Spencer isn't here yet."

She pulled out her phone—he assumed to text her brother—as his parents carefully hurried down the steps.

This was usually a happy moment—when he was reunited with his people—but the frustration inside of him nagged. He worked to push it aside.

His mom bounded for him and pulled him into the kind of tight, all-encompassing hug only she could give. She had no idea how much he needed it.

"Good to see you, Mom."

She stepped back, hands on his shoulders and drank him in, tears welling in her eyes. She grabbed his face with her hand. "Ugh, I see the boy I knew in the man that stands before me. You need to shave."

He laughed.

"But you're handsome. You're welcome for that, it's from my side, not your father's."

"What now? Are you making fun of me again?" Will's dad was taking his time up the walk, looking around, probably for a shovel. He was always moving potential obstacles out of his mom's way, and in this case, Will guessed, it was the slipperiness of the snow.

His mom beamed. "You look good." Two pats on his sides and she stepped back. At that, his father moved in, first shaking his hand, then pulling him close in a hug that felt long overdue. He'd missed them.

"Hey, Dad."

His father took a step back. "Ahh. So glad you're home, son."

In their eyes, he saw the man he wanted to be, the man he thought he'd become, but there was a tormenting echo at the back of his mind chanting *people don't change.*

"Lauren." Mom turned to her. "Oh, my goodness. You are a *stunner!* Steve, look at Lauren," she said, waving her hand in Lauren's general direction. "She's even more beautiful than I remember!"

That's an understatement.

"Kath, that's weird, and it's cold, let's get these guys inside." His father rubbed his hands together, then turned toward their guest. "Hi, Lauren, and yes, she's right, you look great."

Lauren blushed, and Will longed for her. He wanted to take her somewhere quiet to apologize again and to ask how he could make it up to her.

"It's good to see you both," Lauren said. "I texted my brother. He's supposed to be here to pick me up."

"Come inside." Will's mom waved a hand at the car. "Just leave your bags in the car, and we'll go in and eat. Everyone's here for the holidays, so I apologize in advance— it's going to be noisy."

Lauren looked a little panicked. "I don't want to impose."

"Nonsense." His mom wrapped her arm around Lauren's shoulders, then led her up the sidewalk to the door. "We love company! And I made more food than we will ever eat in a lifetime."

"You obviously haven't seen Will eat lately," Lauren said with a wry smile.

Lauren glanced back at Will. He held her gaze for a beat, tried to smile, then he looked away. She was trying to lighten the mood, but he was in pretty deep. His mom led Lauren into the house, and Will and his father hung back.

"Uh-oh," his dad said under his breath.

Will frowned. "What? What's uh-oh?"

"What's going on there?" His father nodded toward Lauren.

"Where?"

His dad looked amused. "No one told me that my eyes would stop working when I got older." He wiped his glasses with the bottom of his shirt and looked up through them to see if they were clean. "But I'm not blind."

"It's. . .nothing," Will sighed. "There is absolutely nothing going on there."

Dad slung an arm around him and patted his shoulder. "Uh huh."

They walked toward the door, and the cinnamon aroma of his mom's famous wassail rushed out to meet him.

"How's Pops?" Will asked.

Now Dad sighed. "It's good you came when you did."

Sadness pulled at his edges as the image of his grandfather, strong and vibrant, raced through his mind.

"He'll be happy to see you, that's for sure."

Will stopped at the threshold of the house and decided to stop wallowing. This Christmas wasn't about him, or the love he'd never had and still managed somehow to lose. It was about his family, about their traditions, and sadly, about having the courage to say goodbye.

CHAPTER 29

❄

The moment Lauren stepped into the Sinclair house, she felt like she was inside a real-life Norman Rockwell painting.

Arguments about licking the spoon, laughter over whose hand was under whose at Slap, she could practically *see* the smell lines coming off the steaming platters of food set out on the oversized, handmade oak table.

A fleeting memory of the last time she was in this home hung at the back of her mind, but she quickly pushed it aside, choosing instead to relish this moment, in the here and now.

Instantly, the house felt like home.

"Lauren, you must be exhausted," Will's mom said. Then, half whispering, "I can't believe you made it this whole way with Will as your driver."

"Mom, I can still hear you!" Will called from the hallway entrance. It sounded like he had lightened up a bit after coming inside. Looking around the room, she could see why.

"Come in, I know you've been sitting in a car for a week, but sit down, sit down." She ushered Lauren into the living room, which was full of people who stopped chattering at the sight of her.

"Everyone, this is Lauren," Mrs. Sinclair said. "Lauren, this is Nadia, Kayla, Kayla's husband Mark, her son Captain Louie and Will's grandfather, my dad, is over there sleeping in the recliner."

Lauren followed the line-up, trying to remember everyone's names.

"Nadia's husband Paul is making his *famous* lasagna in the kitchen," Will's mom added.

"And I made the back-up lasagna this morning for when Paul's goes up in flames." Nadia shot her a knowing look, and Lauren laughed.

"Will didn't tell us he was bringing someone home." Kayla shifted her son on her lap and glanced at Nadia.

"Will never brings *anyone* home," Mark said, stuffing caramel corn in his mouth.

Will's mom smiled at Lauren, relishing in some inside knowledge. "He told *me*."

"Oh, I just got a ride," Lauren said. "I'm Spencer's sister."

"Wait. Spencer Richmond?" Nadia asked.

Lauren nodded.

"No way!"

Another nod.

"Spencer was always the cutest of all of Will's friends," Nadia said.

"Definitely," Kayla agreed. "You live in California too?"

"Yeah, I work in TV. Set decoration."

Both of Will's sisters *ooh'd* and *ahh'd* at that, and Lauren resisted the urge to downplay it. She thought her job was pretty cool, and it made her happy other people agreed.

Mrs. Sinclair reached out. "Lauren, let me take your coat."

Lauren shrugged it off and handed it over.

"And for the record, you can call me Kathy." She started back the way they'd come in just as Will and his dad appeared in the doorway of the living room.

Both Nadia and Kayla jumped up, rushing toward their brother. One jumped on his back and the other latched on to his leg. These were grown women with husbands. Will trudged in the room, dragging one like a kid going for a ride on the hardwood floor.

Lauren took a step back, marveling at the sight of a family that loved well.

A strong pang of jealousy shot through her, and she shoved it off.

I'm fine by myself! I've got Maddie and a promotion, I'm totally fine!

And still, the sight of Will's nephew running headlong into Will's stomach. reaching for him and Will tossing the toddler in the air set something off inside of her.

She looked away, feeling out of place.

"Lauren, how was the drive?" Will's dad asked.

Her eyes darted to Will's, then away. "It was, uh, good. You know, some stops along the way, some 'speed bumps,'" she put speed bumps in air quotes, "but you know, we made good time, and..."

Shut up! Shut up! Shut up!

"...I got to...ahem...see a lot of cool... things."

Lauren thought she actually heard crickets.

"Good," Steve said, saving her. "I hope you're staying for dinner. Pauly's lasagna is the stuff of legend."

Nadia caught Lauren's eye and mouthed *'No it's not'* while shaking her head slowly. Everyone laughed, and a voice from the kitchen shouted, "Are you talking about me? I promise this time it's going to be good!"

This time, both Nadia and Kayla cut their hands back and forth across their throats, mouthing, *'No it isn't.'*

"Last Christmas, Paul decided to make lasagna." Nadia

lowered her voice, telling the whole room the story for what she imagined was the umpteenth time. "But there was a football game on, and he forgot about it, and when he finally remembered, it was a black lump in the oven."

"If you breathe in deep, you can still smell the smoke in the curtains," Kathy laughed. "I should replace them."

"But Mom insisted we all pretend it was still edible," Will added. "So we didn't hurt Paul's feelings."

"It was the most disgusting thing I've ever eaten," Mark said dryly, looking back at the kitchen to make sure he wasn't heard.

A tall, thin man with a thick beard and a full head of dark hair stepped into the doorway of what Lauren assumed was the kitchen. He wore a frilly pink apron over his tan sweater and no shoes. "While I appreciate the pity meal last year," he swatted Nadia with a towel, "this time, I am confident I will not fail." He glanced at Lauren. "You're new. Impressionable. Don't be swayed by their horrible, horrible lies."

"It's the truth, Lauren, you've been warned!" Nadia quipped.

She smiled. She instantly liked these people—their familial banter was different than what she was used to. It wasn't intended to leave scars.

She glanced at Will and saw that the sea of people had parted, clearing his line of sight to the other side of the room. His attention laser-focused on his grandpa, sitting in the chair, eyes fluttering open. The old man had an afghan over his lap and an oxygen mask affixed over his nose. Will looked stricken.

Was this the same grandpa he'd told her about? The man Will had let down all those years ago?

"Pops." Will's voice was a whisper.

"Will?" The old man's voice was hoarse and quiet as he reached for his grandson.

Will crossed the room and leaned in to hug the frail man. The others drifted together, as if moved by the scene before them. Kathy sniffed and wiped her eyes. She glanced over at

Lauren, who felt every bit the intruder. This moment felt private, too private, for her to be a part of it.

But Kathy was at her side in seconds, as if intent on not letting Lauren feel out of place. She leaned closer. "Will's grandpa is very special to him. Did he tell you about Pops at all?"

Lauren thought back to a stop on the road trip, his admission at the torchlight parade. "A little bit."

Will had mentioned his regret over disappointing his grandpa, but he'd downplayed how much his grandpa meant to him.

Kathy motioned for Lauren to follow her through the entryway and into a den on the opposite side of the front door. One entire wall was made up of bookshelves, stacked to the ceiling with books. Lauren gasped. "Okay, this is my favorite room, ever."

Kathy smiled. "Oh! Are you a reader?"

She nodded in awe. "Huge."

"I knew I liked you."

Lauren blushed at the compliment.

"You're welcome to borrow anything from my library," Kathy said. "As long as you agree to tell me what you think when you've finished."

Lauren nodded. "Deal."

Kathy paused. "I would really like that, actually."

She smiled, tilting her head. "Me too."

"Anyway, that's not why I brought you in here, though I could talk about books all night long." She knelt and pulled out a large red photo album.

The album said *Will* on the front in script-y handwriting. Kathy lovingly ran her hand over the word.

Lauren thought it strange that she was sitting with Will's mom, about to get a peek into what she assumed were captured moments of his childhood. She would've *flipped* over this when she was younger. But now, everything was just —different.

Will said he liked me. Why couldn't I have just said, 'I like you too' like a normal person? How different would things be if she had?

But no. This was better. This was the best thing for her heart. At least that's what she was telling herself.

Kathy flipped the photo album open. "Don't ever tell him I'm showing you this."

Lauren stifled a giggle. It was nice to have a secret with Will's mom. It was nice to have a secret with *any* mom. Kathy flipped through the pages quickly, and Lauren almost asked her to slow down. In spite of everything, she still wanted to know everything about him.

She stopped on a page and pointed to a photo of a very young Will, gap-toothed, sitting on the shoulders of an older man. Will's arms were wrapped around his forehead. "Will and Pops after Will's first baseball game. Pops was *always* convinced Will was something special. Said he had a gift. Nobody ever believed in a kid more." She flipped the page. "He was the one who taught Will how to pitch. Coached his Little League teams. Studied videos of Will's form when he started having trouble with his elbow in tenth grade and then came up with a plan to correct it."

Another page. A slightly out-of-focus shot of Will, on the mound, mid-pitch. "Will making varsity as a Freshman. He only pitched a few games that year, but he won every single one of them."

She turned a few pages and stopped again, and this page had a newspaper story clipped to the top. Lots of pictures of Will behind a microphone, shaking hands, holding up a collegiate jersey with his name on the back.

"Will on College Commitment Day." Kathy touched one of the photos.

"I remember that." Lauren admired Will's smile in the one

where he was holding up the jersey. His mouth was open, grinning, like he couldn't believe what was happening.

She turned the page. These pictures were of Will, but none on or near a baseball field. One giving a peace sign with a few other guys, one of him making muscles in a kitchen.

"This was just after Will lost his scholarship. I think it broke my dad's heart."

Lauren glanced at Kathy, her eyes glistening with fresh tears.

"Broke all of our hearts. It was just so hard to see him go through it." She stilled. "Will isn't like that anymore, you know."

Lauren looked at the images in the open album in Kathy's lap. She didn't know what had happened to make this sweet kid with the big smile and a family that did nothing but support him make such terrible choices, but she hoped his mom was right. For their sakes.

"How do you know he's not like that anymore?" she asked quietly.

Kathy flipped the page. "Because he knows how much he hurt everyone, especially Pops. And he promised he'd never do that again. He's lucky he got a second chance, but I think a part of him will always regret what his choices cost him."

Will had said as much.

Lauren's gaze fell to one of the photos on the page. It was Will and his grandpa, standing outside a restaurant with a large sign in the background that read *Pop's Diner*. She pointed to it. "Where was this taken?"

Kathy squinted at it, but before she could answer, Nadia walked in the room.

"Mom, you should come back." She gestured excitedly. "Will's giving Pops his gift."

"Okay." Kathy closed the album and stood as Nadia rushed off. Will's mom smiled at Lauren. "Thanks for doing this trip with him. I know it couldn't have been easy on him, and I think it helped having you there."

Lauren frowned. She didn't understand, and Kathy didn't give her a chance to ask for clarification. She stood and ushered Lauren into the living room. Over her shoulder, she asked, "Did you help Will with the gift?"

The question flustered her. "No, I. . .didn't know anything about it."

Kathy smiled, and Lauren thought she was just the kind of mother Lauren had always wished she'd had. A gnawing, raw feeling came over her at the realization.

She hung back for a single moment, looking longingly at the red photo album and wishing she could go back to the beginning and learn every story behind every photo inside.

She had a feeling there was a lot more to Will that had yet to be revealed.

CHAPTER 30

❄

Lauren followed Kathy into the living room. The older woman sat with the others on the sofa, between Will and Nadia, who simultaneously laid their heads on their mom's shoulders. Kathy gave them each a pat on the cheeks, and said, "Aww, my wonderful children..."

Lauren loved that.

Will's Dad stood behind the couch next to both of his sons-in-law, and Kayla and Captain Louie perched on the loveseat. Lauren stayed off to the side, in the doorway.

Everyone faced the television. Will's computer was positioned on the coffee table, cords coming out of it connected to the back of the TV.

Kathy reached an open hand. "Lauren, come sit." She moved over to make room between her and Will. He looked over, meeting her eyes, and she could see now that there was pain in his.

Pops was clearly sick, in his last days, she suspected, and it was obvious to her that this was devastating to all of them. She could see that it was especially devastating to Will.

Her heart grieved that he was hurting. He hadn't said a word.

She moved through the room and sat gingerly on the edge of the sofa. Someone turned the lights off, and Will took over from there.

He cleared his throat. "As you all know, when I was ten years old, Pops and I went on an epic adventure. A journey across the country because Pops thought I needed a little history lesson, and an appreciation of the way things used to be done."

"That trip wasn't really about the open highway or all the places we stopped on the way, though, was it Pops?" Will paused and looked at his grandpa.

Pops pulled the mask off his face and smiled. "That trip," a breath, "was about," another breath, then a toothy smile, "you and me, kiddo."

"That's true," Will said. "It was a chance for a kid to get to know his grandpa, who turned out to be a pretty great guy. Crazy driver, I think I learned a few swear words on that trip. . .but pretty great nonetheless." The room laughed in acknowledgement, with Nadia adding, "He nearly killed us that one time speeding over the hill on Sink Hollow Road, do you remember that?"

More laughter.

Will picked up his laptop, hit a few buttons and a photo appeared on the television. Ten-year-old Will and Pops, standing in front of one of the vintage gas stations she was pretty sure she'd seen on the way here.

"We always said we were going to do it again," Will said. "So, this year, on the way home for Christmas," Will's voice broke, just slightly, "I decided to take that trip in your honor, Pops."

That's why. Oh, my goodness, Will.

"I wanted to revisit as many of the same places as I could remember. So, in honor of the best grandpa a kid could ever ask for, here is a recap of our cross-country Christmas road trip adventure."

He gave a quick glance at Lauren, then focused—as they all did—on the screen.

And right there, moment for moment, their road trip played out in front of them.

Image after image of Will posing at historical landmarks, vintage gas stations, the world's largest rocking chair, and out in front of their hotels. Big Mom's Wigwam. Pop's Diner. The Torchlight Parade. All these images capturing so much more, she realized now, than a simple road trip home.

Scattered throughout were photos of Lauren. Lauren walking to the car. The one she took of Will watching the sunset on the side of the road. Lauren and Rosa in the kitchen. Lauren at the Christmas market. Lauren asleep in the car with her mouth wide open.

Mortified! Will!

Will standing by the New Mexico sign. Will changing the flat tire.

And on and on. Photo after photo documenting the last several days. Documenting her many mixed feelings when it came to Will.

She'd been so terrible to him about this trip. She'd complained that he wanted to take his time or make several stops along the way, and once again, she was ashamed. He hadn't done it to get under her skin—he'd done it all for his grandfather.

And it couldn't have been easy.

Lauren tried to swallow around the ball of emotion, but couldn't keep her eyes from welling with tears. Why hadn't he said anything?

Then came the picture of the two of them, with Santa, where she wasn't even looking at the camera. . .but at him.

Lauren pretended not to notice, but Will's parents raised their eyebrows at each other in an unspoken conversation.

The last picture was taken of the rearview mirror, and in the mirror was a vintage highway marker with the road stretched out to the horizon. The picture had gotten the road ahead and the road behind in the same shot.

The road ahead and the road behind.

By the end, Will had gone silent, his entertaining narration finished. She reached over and slipped her hand around his and squeezed, wishing she could go back to the beginning of the week with this new knowledge, with the truth about who he really was, and take the entire trip again. She'd do so many things differently.

He squeezed back.

Someone flipped the lights back on, and the room was filled with sniffles, warm smiles through tears, and the kind of looks you only experience when you're part of a tight-knit family. Will held her hand for a few seconds longer, then pulled away, turning toward his grandpa.

"Lauren, what was your favorite part of the trip?" Kayla asked. "We were always jealous because we never got to go. It was a guys-only thing." She rolled her eyes playfully.

"I always wanted to see those upside-down Cadillacs sticking out of the ground—did you see those?" Nadia asked.

So many moments from their road trip crashed into Lauren's mind at that question.

"He said you like. . .uh. . .white chocolate mocha?" Will, holding out her favorite drink.

"C'mon, I'm a catch." Will, showing a mouthful of French toast.

"The first time I kiss this woman is going to be because I want to— not because some tradition told me I had to." Will, under Melinda's mistletoe.

"That's awesome! Really, really exciting! Are you excited?" Will, smiling about her artwork.

"*Jackson. You know we have to talk about a few things, right?*" *Will, sitting on the edge of the armchair, leaning toward his player.*

"*This spot has your name written all over it.*" *Will, on an inner tube, ready to sled down the side of the mountain.*

And then, another memory, plucked straight from the day she met Will for the first time.

"*You can have mine.*" *She held out her Coke in front of the fridge in the kitchen.*

It may as well have been her heart she was holding out to him.

She realized she'd paused slightly longer than she should've. "It's hard to choose just one."

"Okay, then tell us all of your favorites." Kayla smiled at her.

And just like that, Lauren was one of them. She told them about the trip, surprised at how much she remembered. She told them about the furry spider in her room, about Will talking with his mouth full of food, his off-key singing, Big Mama's butt hanging out of the wigwam, the Christmas Ball that almost was (*she even put the part in there about Gin, to which both sisters rolled their eyes*)—she gushed about everything.

When Paul called out "Dinner's ready!" Lauren was almost sad to see their conversation come to an end. She'd never had sisters, and while she loved Spencer, she hadn't known what she was missing.

She liked the way it felt to be included.

Someone had set an extra place for her at the table, and though she should probably check her phone to find out where her brother was, she found herself wanting to stay right there, in the middle of this family.

As if somehow, that made her a part of something special too.

CHAPTER 31

They'd just finished eating when Kathy hopped up from her seat with a cheerful, "It's time for dessert."

"Oh, Mom, no—" Will held up a hand, but his mother waved him off.

"You sit down, young man," she said. "We took care of everything." She winked at him, and Lauren felt—not saw—his shoulders slump in an emotion she couldn't name.

As far as she knew, Will didn't have anything against dessert.

His dad clapped his hands together and nodded at his son-in-law. "Mark, would you hit the lights?"

Mark flicked the switch on the wall, and only the white twinkle lights of the Christmas tree in the corner remained. Lauren assumed this was some sort of Sinclair family tradition, but when Kathy returned to the dining room, she carried a cake, candles flickering on top of it.

The entire room erupted in a rousing rendition of "Happy Birthday." Nobody had mentioned a birthday—who were they singing to? She visually circled the table, and she realized they were all looking at her.

Kathy grinned as she set the cake down in front of her, the chorus of "Happy Birthday, dear Lauren," filling the room. Lauren shook her head. It wasn't her birthday—why were they—and then she looked down at the cake.

The head of a beautiful frosted pony stared back at her.

The song ended, and Will's family erupted in cheers. The pony went blurry as Lauren's eyes filled with tears. He got her a birthday cake?

A pony cake.

With twelve flickering candles.

"Make a wish and blow out the candles, Lauren," Kathy said once the commotion died down.

Lauren looked up at her and a tear slid down her cheek.

"Oh, no." Will's mom brought a hand to her heart.

Lauren held up a hand. "I'm sorry. It's," she didn't know if she could finish, "it's just been a really long time since I had a birthday cake." The last part came out as a whisper.

"We know it's not really your birthday." Will's mom looked around at the others in the room. "But Will told about your wish to Santa, and he really wanted to make it come true."

She felt Will shift.

He leaned toward her. "I'm sorry—"

"No, it's. . ." She didn't have the words. "It's the nicest thing anyone's ever done for me." She wiped her cheeks.

"Wait. It was *Will's* idea?" Nadia asked, surprised. "You didn't mention that when you were stealthily cluing us all in on your plan on the way to the dinner table."

"Our brother, the ro*man*tic." Kayla exchanged a look with her sister that said "aww".

"I asked for brothers, mom. *Brothers.*" Will said, obviously embarrassed.

"Blow out the candles, Lauren," Kayla said from across the table, bouncing her son on her lap. "Captain Louie here is dying to try that cake."

Lauren closed her eyes, but when she tried to think of something to wish for, she came up empty. She couldn't have dreamed up a more perfect moment. This was more than enough for her, though she did wish things were different between her and Will. That would be her wish.

She blew out the candles and again, Will's family erupted in cheers.

So, this was what it was like to have a family. She looked around the table as they all jumped into action, clearing dinner plates, cutting the cake and handing it out on small, turquoise plates. She got the first piece and requested a corner, the one with the most frosting. They talked and laughed and told years-old Christmas stories, looping Lauren in on everything Sinclair, and it couldn't have been a more perfect night.

Except, she realized, for the very somber, very quiet man at her side.

After they'd all finished their legitimately tasty dinner (compliments to Paul!) and the surprise dessert that Lauren would never forget, she helped clear the table. She and Nadia stood at the kitchen sink, scraping and rinsing plates to be filed into the dishwasher when she spotted Will out in the big backyard through the window above the sink. He sat in an Adirondack chair positioned around a firepit, his back to the house.

Nadia followed her gaze, then looked at Lauren. "What's going on with you two?"

"Oh, nothing," Lauren said. "We're just friends."

"Friends, my eye," Nadia said.

Lauren frowned.

"Yeah, I've *never* seen him look at anyone the way he looks at you." Kayla was scooping leftovers into plastic containers, and said this as Kathy was entering the room.

"That's a fact," Will's mom said.

"I promise, we're just friends," Lauren said, hoping that they were at least that.

"But you like him," Nadia said matter-of-factly.

Lauren started to protest, but Nadia pointed an ice cream scoop at her, eyebrows raised, head cocked, daring her to deny it.

"He needs someone like you." Kayla bumped her with her shoulder. "Someone who won't let him slack off."

"Someone who forces him to reach his full potential." Nadia's statement made Lauren think this wasn't the first time they'd all had this conversation.

Kathy leaned forward for a better look of her son. "He still punishes himself for mistakes that are almost a decade old." She dried her hands on a towel. "Ugh, that boy. I wish he understood the concept of grace."

Lauren went still.

She certainly hadn't helped with that, throwing old mistakes at him like a pitcher on a mound.

Her eyes wandered back into the yard, where Will sat, hands folded on his lap, looking up at the sky. "What's he doing out there?"

"Oh, that's his 'thinking spot.'" Kayla moved to Lauren's other side. "He always said it was too loud in the house. . ."

"Too loud? What*ever*!" Nadia said, too loudly.

Kayla continued, ". . .so he had to go out there to get any real thinking done."

"What do you think he's thinking about?" Lauren asked.

"You," they all three said in unison. They erupted in laughter, and Lauren's face flushed in embarrassment.

"Leave the dishes, Lauren," Kathy said. "Go talk to him. Put him out of his misery or make him the happiest guy alive."

"I'm telling you, you've got it all wrong." She paused. "But I do need to talk to him, so—it's okay if I go?"

The three, almost choreographed, looked at one another and laughed. Kathy shooed her out the door, and Lauren hoped she could figure out what on earth to say when she came face-to-face with this man who had completely, utterly, and wholly stolen her heart.

Again.

CHAPTER 32

❄

Being home was harder this year than ever before. His parents' house was instant comfort, like an oasis, like a rest stop after miles on his weary soul, but seeing Pops in his current state—well, he wasn't prepared.

To make matters worse, the tension between him and Lauren had his stomach in knots. He wanted to make things right with her, but he had no idea where to begin.

Profound sadness wound its way through his stomach, wrapping around his heart like a snake.

The house was situated in the country, out on the edge of Pleasant Valley, and his mom sure knew how to make a holiday special. She didn't just decorate a tree or a single room—every single nook and cranny of the house had been transformed. His room would undoubtedly have white lights strung up around the ceiling, and each room had its own tree. His was decorated with baseball ornaments and those popsicle stick ones he'd made at a camp one summer.

He loved being here, especially during the holidays.

His mind wandered back over the road trip and all the little ways Lauren had managed to capture his attention without even trying. He hadn't told her, but after he found out about her promotion, he sent the email she'd helped him craft to his boss—he was putting himself out there. He might not deserve it, but she inspired him to want more.

And he wanted more from Lauren, too, despite everything. But he wasn't confident she felt the same.

He turned toward the sound of a door opening, then closing, and saw Lauren, wrapped up in her winter coat and wearing an old pink stocking cap he was pretty sure his mother had forced her to put on. She stuffed her hands in her pockets and made her way to where he sat.

Neither of them said anything, both staring over the yard, where, in the distance, he could see the moonlight reflecting on the river.

"I'm really sorry about your grandpa," she finally said.

He hated that he couldn't respond—his voice wouldn't have held up.

"You didn't say anything about his health or why you were really taking this trip."

He blew out a breath. "It's hard to talk about."

She stilled. "Are you okay?"

No. I'm not.

For a million reasons, he wasn't okay.

"That cake, I—" She sat next to him.

"Maybe I should've canceled it." While he'd really wanted to be the one to make that wish come true for her, the gesture felt misguided in light of what he'd discovered about their history.

"Why?" She faced him. "I meant what I said—it was the nicest thing anyone's ever done for me. You took a twelve-year-old girl's dream and made it come true." She paused. "Thank you."

He kept his gaze fixed on the yard, the trees, anything but her. "It hardly makes up for—"

"Things are strange between us now," she cut in, then paused. "I don't like it."

He glanced at her. "I don't like it either."

"I'm sorry I ever told you what happened at that party." She sighed, and rethought that. "Actually, that's not true. I'm glad I told you because I needed to get it out there, but I'm sorry it put this wedge between us."

"You shouldn't be the one apologizing," he said. "It's good for me to remember sometimes how my actions affected other people. I was so selfish. So stupid. I hurt everyone who loved me."

"But you're not that guy anymore."

He scoffed.

"I really believe that, Will, and your family believes it too." He caught the edge of her smile in the blue light of the moon. "They're all so proud of you—and they should be. You didn't let your mistakes ruin your life."

"They wouldn't have let me," he said.

"You're so lucky to have them. You don't even know." She went still at that. "Or. . .maybe you do. You were over enough at my house to see how messed up things were there."

He didn't answer—but yeah, he knew.

"If I had a family like yours, I'd love coming home for Christmas, too."

He smiled. "They're pretty great." They both glanced toward the house, and Lauren half-expected to find the three women still standing in the kitchen, watching them.

Instead, they saw an empty room, a single light over the kitchen sink.

He turned back to her. "And they love you."

She looked up at him. "Really?"

"Since we got home, every single person in that house has found a way to tell me how great you are. And three of them made sure to add, 'If you screw this up, you're an idiot.'"

She giggled, and then, her smile faded. "You know, Will, I've kept my heart all locked up for most of my adult life."

"Because of me?"

"Not entirely. I think it had a lot to do with my family." She went still. "But also because of you."

"You have no idea how much I hate that," he said.

"I'm not telling you that so you'll feel bad. I just think you need to understand the whole picture. I don't ever put myself in a situation where I might get hurt." She kicked at something invisible, her shoe leaving an imprint in the thin layer of freshly fallen snow. "I don't like taking risks on anyone other than myself, and only then when I've done so much research it doesn't feel risky anymore. I focus on the things I can control. I date guys I have no real interest in because I know they can't hurt me. I'm perfectly content to spend my weekends working or reading or reading about my work."

She turned toward him. "But I realize now that some things —some *people*—are worth the risk."

He searched her eyes, his heart racing hopefully. "Lauren, what are you saying?"

"I'm saying I know being confronted with our past can be a lot, and yes, we have some history—but I believe in second chances."

He struggled to not let his emotions show. "I don't deserve your forgiveness, Lauren."

"Nobody deserves forgiveness, Will. That's the point. That's what grace is."

"You sound like my mom." He chuckled. "One of her favorite things to say is, 'there's grace for that.'" His face turned serious. "But is there really? Is there grace for someone who's made so many mistakes?"

She reached over and took his hand.

She inhaled a deep, slow breath. "You and me, Sinclair. Something about it just works."

"You and me?"

She nodded. "It's all we need."

He reached for her. "I'm going to kiss you now."

"Well, stop talking about it and do it already, wou—?"

And he did.

In that moment, he really did feel invincible. She made him think he could do anything. She inspired him to do better, to *be* better. And he wanted to experience it all with her.

He leaned toward her and took her face in his hands, then they both stood, her arms circling his waist. The heat from her body melded with his, even through their winter coats, and he couldn't think of any reason not to follow his heart.

She inched up on her tiptoes, and he dipped down, savoring the moment. Her skin was cold, but her mouth was warm, and as he deepened the kiss, the rest of the world melted away.

He pulled back and looked at her, hands still framing her face. "I've wanted to do that practically since I picked you up in that diner on the pier."

She smiled up at him. "Was it worth the wait?"

"So worth it." He leaned in and pressed a soft kiss to her forehead. "But there's always room for improvement, so I think we're going to need a lot of practice." Another kiss, one he hoped communicated that this moment made him feel like the luckiest man alive.

She unwound her arms from around him and pressed her hands to his chest. "Something to look forward to."

The back door flung open, and his mother raced out, cordless phone in her hand. "Lauren, it's your brother! They're having their baby!"

Lauren's eyes widened. "Wait. What? Now!?"

"He said he's been trying to call you all night," Mom said. "They're at the hospital now!"

"Let's go." Will led her back into the house, where they were met with a chorus of voices shouting at them to send pictures when the baby arrived. Lauren thanked them the whole way out the door, and as they turned to go, Will stole a glimpse into the living room, where his grandfather was resting in his chair.

He met Will's eyes from the across the room and gave him a thumbs-up.

The road ahead and the road behind.

He crossed the room and squeezed his grandpa's hand. "Merry Christmas, Pops. And thanks for believing in me. Even when I didn't believe in myself."

Pops nodded, then pulled off the oxygen mask. He spoke with a huge smile plastered on his face. "Get that girl to the hospital, would ya? Want me to drive?"

CHAPTER 33

❄

Back in the familiar space of Will's Jeep, Lauren felt herself finally relax.

She couldn't have predicted that a crazy cross-country road trip would've made her a lover of Christmas, but here she was, basking in its glow.

Will reached across the seat and took her hand, holding it like it was something that required great care. He drove a little faster than usual, getting to the hospital in record time, despite the snow.

He turned off the engine and pressed her knuckles to his lips. His very full, very kissable lips.

"Listen, maybe let me tell Spencer about us," he said.

She frowned. "Okay."

"He was really protective of you," Will said. "And I owe him a lot. You said I picked myself up after everything that happened, but I couldn't' have done it without Spencer's help."

She had no trouble believing that was true. Her brother had always been fiercely loyal to his friends.

Will went on. "One time he told me that in a lot of ways, you were the only family he really had."

Lauren stilled. It was true, wasn't it? With two completely unreliable and self-absorbed parents, she and Spencer had made their own way. She was important to him—he made sure she knew that, and how had she repaid him? With distance and unanswered text messages.

"You know, after seeing your family together I realize how important people are," she said. "I think because of the way I processed everything with my parents, I have a tendency to push people away."

"You?" Will feigned surprise. "No."

She shoved his shoulder, and he grabbed her wrist, coming in for another kiss, which she was more than happy to give. She couldn't be sure, but she thought it was quite possible she'd be perfectly content to kiss him for hours and hours.

"Wow, I really love kissing you," he said when he pulled away. "I'm going to fall asleep dreaming about it, you know that, right?"

She grinned and opened her car door. "Good. My goal is to bewitch you, body and soul."

"Ooh, a *Pride and Prejudice* deep cut. I like it."

They walked through the sliding doors of the hospital, figured out where they were going, and made their way to the elevator. Lauren was still woozy from his kisses, but not so light-headed that she wasn't ready for more.

When the doors of the elevator closed, she felt his arms around her again. She couldn't remember a time she'd been quite this happy.

In the quiet of the elevator, Will's kisses felt stolen, exciting, risky. With her back to the wall and her eyes closed, Lauren wished she could freeze time. It took every bit of will power to resist punching the STOP button. His hands wrapped around her waist, and he drew her closer, sending shivers to every nerve-ending in her body. She couldn't believe this was happening. She couldn't believe she was absolutely, one-hundred-percent happy that this was happening.

They were so engrossed in each other they didn't hear the elevator ding. They didn't hear the door open. They didn't notice they were putting on a show for the entire staff on the labor and delivery floor. That is, until they heard someone clear their throat.

"Will?"

Will took a step back, eyes wide at Lauren.

It was Spencer.

They both knew it was, and Lauren had no idea how he was going to feel about any of this. Lauren pressed her lips together to try and hide her smile because the truth was, she loved her brother, and she was going to be a better sister to him than she had been. But she was a grown-up, and he had no say in who she dated.

And she wasn't going to give Will up for anything.

Slowly, Will turned around to face the several pairs of eyes turned in their direction. He lifted a hand in a lame wave. "Hey, Spence."

They stepped out of the elevator, and the doors closed behind them.

Spencer had been standing at the desk talking to one of the nurses, and Lauren only just now realized how tired he looked.

"Spencer," she said. "Is everything okay?"

He looked at her with tears in his eyes and smiled. "Lo, I have a daughter."

Tears sprang to her eyes as her brother pulled her into a tight hug.

"I'm so glad you're here." Then, he reached for Will. "Thanks for getting her home."

"My pleasure," Will said, joining their hug.

"Yeah, you made that obvious." Spencer pulled away, one

hand on each of their arms. "I'm happy to see my plan worked." He grinned.

Lauren and Will exchanged confused glances.

"What do you mean?" she asked.

Spencer started down the hall, motioning for them to follow. "You don't think this was a coincidence, do you?"

Will took her hand as they followed Spencer.

"Lauren had a crush on you forever," Spencer looked at Will.

"You knew about that?" Lauren thought she hid it so well.

"Lauren, please. You wrote 'Mrs. Will Sinclair' all over your diary, and you know I was reading that on the regular." He stopped in front of a hospital room.

"You read my diary?" She crossed her arms and glared at him.

"And Will asked me once, a long time ago, what I'd think if he dated you," Spencer said.

Lauren looked at Will, who, for the first time she could remember, actually blushed. "You did?"

He shrugged. "Spencer said no, so I dropped it."

"You said no!?" Lauren gave her brother a shove.

"He wasn't ready for you, Lo," Spencer said. "He had some growing up to do. But he really turned things around, and I don't know, I started to think maybe you two might finally be ready for each other."

"Spencer Michael Richmond." Lauren said. "I never would've pegged you for a matchmaker."

He shrugged. "What can I say—I have a sixth sense about these things."

"Well, thanks," Will said. "You were right then, and you were right now."

"Good," Spencer said. "Now that we all agree I'm a genius—do you want to meet your niece?"

Lauren beamed. "More than anything."

Inside the room, they found an absolutely radiant Helen,

cradling the sweetest baby with a full head of dark hair. Lauren was unprepared for the wave of emotion that washed over her at the sight of Spencer's little girl.

"Do you want to hold her?" Helen asked.

Lauren nodded. "Yes, please! What's her name?"

"Noel Joy," Spencer said.

Lauren took the baby from her sister-in-law as a tear streamed down her cheek. "She's the most beautiful thing I've ever seen."

Will slipped his arm around her, peering down at her niece, and for the first time since she was ten-years-old, Lauren felt like she had a family again.

What a gift.

The best Christmas gift she could've imagined.

She looked up at Will, whose eyes had filled with tenderness as he pressed a kiss to her forehead. "Do you want to hold her?" she asked.

Will nodded and moved away, reaching for the baby, but Lauren held her just out of his reach. "Before I can hand her over, you have to sing your favorite Christmas carol."

His jaw went slack. "No. No, you aren't throwing this back at me right now—"

She shrugged. "It's just I have something here that smells like heaven and makes you feel like you're the luckiest human in the world, and I *really* want to share it with you, but you have to pay the price."

"I think we will be the ones paying the price, Lauren, have you heard this guy sing?" Spencer laughed.

She narrowed her eyes. "Unfortunately, I have."

"All right," Will said. "You asked for it. In honor of this beautiful child—" he bowed. "There is really only one appropriate Christmas carol." He drew in a breath, then started the heartiest, most horrible, off-key version of "The First Noel" any of them had ever heard.

They all joined in the chorus, even Helen, who laughed the whole way through.

Will took a step back and snapped a photo on his phone—yet another memory of the Christmas Lauren Richmond came back to life.

And as she looked around the room, she couldn't help but count her many, many blessings, and she knew in her heart her days of ignoring Christmas were over.

EPILOGUE

❄

ONE YEAR LATER

"I honestly thought we'd never make it." Lauren had never been so happy to see Will's parents' house as she was at that exact moment. After a full seven days on the road, the two of them had a whole lot of new stories to tell his family around the dinner table.

They'd decided to take the road trip home again in honor of Pops, who'd passed away on New Year's Day almost a year ago, surrounded by his family.

This time, Lauren didn't complain. Not when Will told her he hadn't made any reservations. Not when they made countless unexpected stops. Not even when she got locked in a gas station bathroom and Will didn't come looking for her for a solid thirty-five minutes.

This, she had learned, was part of the adventure of life—and she didn't want to miss a single minute of it.

Inside the coziness of the Sinclair home, they shared photos of their trip, photos of the set of the top-rated sitcom Lauren had decorated, and photos of Will's team, now that he was the head coach.

In the center of the picture of the team was a beaming Jackson Pope.

Spencer and Helen had joined them, along with Noel, who was almost—almost—ready to take her first step. With any luck, it would happen while Lauren was home.

They gathered around the table for Paul's famous lasagna and all at once, Lauren was overcome with emotion. Will took her hand under the table and squeezed it, then leaned in and kissed her cheek. "Well, now. The Christmas spirit suits you."

She smiled. "Yeah, thanks for helping me find it again."

"You know what time it is!" Kathy stood. "Time for dessert." She disappeared into the kitchen, and when she reappeared, holding a tray, Lauren noticed that once again, all eyes were on her. "It's not my birthday."

She turned and found that Will had moved the chair away from the table and now knelt on the floor next to her.

She gasped. "Will?!"

"Lauren, last year when we were here, you told me I was worth taking a risk on. I hope you still feel that way because I'm about to ask you to take an even bigger risk. Only, you can rest assured, there's nothing risky about it at all. I have no doubt in my mind that I'm going to love you for the rest of my life. You're strong and smart and beautiful, and—"

"Oh my gosh, just ask her already!" Spencer said.

Will laughed, and Lauren's eyes welled with tears.

"I wanted to do this surrounded by our family because I know how important they are to both of us—" he shot a look at Spencer— "But I'm kind of regretting that now."

Lauren covered her mouth, laughing. "No, it's perfect."

He reached for a small blue velvet box on the tray his mom had set on the table. He opened it, and inside lay a beautiful platinum ring with a square diamond solitaire that glistened in the light overhead.

"Lauren Richmond." He smiled sweetly at her. "Will you be—"

"YES!" She wrapped her arms around Will just in time for him to say a muffled, "—my wife?"

She pulled back, nodding and smiling as he slipped the ring on her finger.

Around them, Will's sisters were already talking about wedding colors and flowers and locations, but the sound of their voices faded and it was just her and Will, caught in the glow that only something like true love could create.

He leaned in and kissed her, one hand cradling her face, the other still holding her newly adorned hand. When he pulled away, she smiled at him—her future husband—the man she'd loved, then loathed, then loved again.

"Merry Christmas, Will," she said.

"Merry Christmas, future Mrs. Sinclair." Then he pulled her up, took her face in his hands and kissed her like she hoped he'd kiss her every single day for the rest of their lives.

He'd given her the best Christmas gift anyone could have—a family, true love, and a reason to believe in miracles.

THE END

A NOTE FROM THE AUTHOR

Dear Reader,

After writing my first ever Christmas novella, *A Match Made at Christmas,* last year, I knew I would probably want to write a Christmas story every year from now until eternity. I LOVE Christmas, and dreaming up new holiday stories is one of my favorite things to do.

But with this book, it was something else too. I took my first ever intentional break from writing this past summer. I'd taken time off from writing before, but always because some other work project demanded it, and I always felt guilty that I wasn't writing.

But this year, my creativity and motivation had taken a hit, and frankly, I was feeling burned out.

When summer ended, so did my self-imposed writing break, and I knew that in order to fall in love with writing again, I needed a story that was written for one reason—fun.

After the 18+ months we'd all had living in and navigating a pandemic, I just wanted to get lost in a sweet romance for a little while. And maybe that was me not facing reality, or maybe it was simply me coping, I don't know. But either way, the end

A NOTE FROM THE AUTHOR

result is this book, which I've decided I really, really love. And I LOVED writing it.

Like some of you, I was once a young girl with an older brother who had a lot of dreamy friends, so it wasn't too hard to imagine Lauren's story, and creating a character that was her perfect match was pure joy.

While this story is light and fun and Christmasy, it does carry with it an important message—there's grace for our mistakes, and every once in a while, we all need a second chance. What a gift that is, don't you think?

As always, I LOVE to connect with my readers, so I invite you to find and follow me through my newsletter, on social media or in my Facebook Reader Room. I would absolutely love to see you there!

Drop me a line anytime—I love making new friends.

Courtney Walsh

courtney@courtneywalshwrites.com

ACKNOWLEDGMENTS

Adam—Without you, Will's flirtatiousness would've come across as awkward and unbelievable (because, anyone who knows me knows flirting isn't part of my personality.) Thank you also for being my first reader, my editor, my business partner, my constant cheerleader and one of the best human beings I've ever met.
Me + You.

My kids, Sophia, Ethan & Sam—Because you are some of my favorite people in the world, and because you don't give me much grief for being a terrible cook and homemaker.

Becky Wade & Katie Ganshert—Friends who are more like family. For the brainstorming, the laughing, the crying, the dreaming, the learning…I am eternally thankful for you both.

Melissa Tagg—For always understanding the struggle of living (and loving) two very different lives. And for letting me ramble about my workouts. I adore you.

My Mom, Cindy Fassler—Thank you for always cheering me on so genuinely. You are the kind of mother I always hope I can be…but I think I'm a little too selfish to get there.

Our Studio Kids & Families—Do you have any idea how special you are? You make my "day job" nothing but pure joy. I'm so thankful for each one of you!

Denise Hershberger—Thank you for helping me with Rosa's Spanish. And for being SUCH an encouragement to me.

My Brother, Chad Fassler—for having such cute friends in high school. ;)

ABOUT THE AUTHOR

Courtney Walsh is the Carol award-winning author of fifteen novels and two novellas. Her debut novel, *A Sweethaven Summer*, was a *New York Times* and *USA Today* e-book best-seller and a Carol Award finalist in the debut author category. In addition, she has written two craft books and several full-length musicals. Courtney lives with her husband and three children in Illinois, where she co-owns a performing arts studio and youth theatre with the best business partner she could imagine—her husband.

Visit her online at www.courtneywalshwrites.com

Printed in France by Amazon
Brétigny-sur-Orge, FR